Ryan Dennis is a former Fulbright Scholar in Creative Writing and has taught creative writing at several universities. He has been published in various literary journals, particularly in the US, including The Cimarron Review, The Threepenny Review and New England Review. In addition to completing a PhD in creative writing at the National University of Ireland, Galway, he is a syndicated columnist for agricultural journals around the world.

The Beasts They Turned Away is Ryan's debut novel.

THE BEASTS THEY TURNED AWAY

RYAN DENNIS

époque press

Published by **époque press** in 2021

www.epoquepress.com

The right of Ryan Dennis to be identified as the
author of this work has been asserted in accordance
with section 77 of the Copyright, Designs and
Patents Act 1988.

Typeset in Gotham Light / Medium
& Dazzle Unicase Medium

Typesetting & cover design by **Ten Storeys®**

Printed and bound in Great Britain by Clays Ltd, Elcograf S.p.A.

British Library Cataloguing-in-Publication Data
A catalogue record for this book is available from
the British Library

ISBN 978-1-9998960-8-9

To my father,
who stands mythic in his own right.

THE DEAD PILE

The old man and the child are in the Ford, the child sits on the floor, tucked in by the steering column. A wilted cow hangs from the bucket. It is the whole of what is in front of them, pushing and pulling on the weight of the machine. When the tractor is not steady the beast swings against the grill, its hind legs flinching. The image of the old man and the child reflected in the glass. Cast against the dead animal. The old man looks at the child's reflection. The child's reflection looks back.

The Ford follows the hedgerow, traces the ruts that lay before it. They lead into a stand of willows and brush. Tangles of dried grass brush along the hooves of the cow. The bones in the grass snap, shatter beneath the wheels of the tractor. The tractor passes between two willows, the drooping archway they make, the cow swinging below it. Swollen eyes to the east, its head dragging on the ground.

The bucket drops, the engine falls in pitch and the old man turns it off before climbing out. Offers a hand to the child but the child lowers himself off the steps, obstinate. Walks ahead.

The ground below the willows is mounded like plagued flesh, the limbs of the dead pulled from it by the foxes and mice to have the murky tissue cleaned from them. The white hollow faces of cows stare out of the brush and leaf litter around them, looking at the old man, the child. Open-jawed, calling out to them. The silent chorus they make. The old man

1

looses the chain from the animal in front of the loader, throws the chain into the bucket.

The child walks through the dead pile. He picks up a leg bone, throws it against the bark of a tree. The old man sits on a soil heap, leans on his knees. Watches the child. The canopy above, thick with leaf cover, seals out the light of the day, puts the remains in perpetual twilight. In the goldenrod at his feet is a number, half-sunken in the earth, on red plastic. He pulls on it, draws the neck strap out of the ground with it, where it had been swelling in the clay. 417. He remembers there was a 417, and that is something. He balls it in his pocket, where it bulges. There will be another 417. A resurrection, the only one possible under this dark bend of willow trees.

The child stands over the cow. The cow gazes back, taut bursting eyes. The child hits the cow.

Hey there, the old man says.

The child swings his fist and it lands in the soft flesh of the cow's neck.

What are you on about, Child? Stop that now.

The child pulls on its ear and then slaps it in the ribs. Her chest echoes, empty. He leans back and kicks her in the muzzle.

The old man chuckles and then shakes his head and then stands up. Will you stop that?

The child stomps on the cow's hoof, which lays curled over tyre tracks. Nearly falls as he jumps on it.

The old man grabs the child's shirt, pulls him against his body. Don't, he says. Puts his arms around him tightly. Again whispers, don't.

The child leans from him, swinging his arms. Breath-heavy. Rams his head against the old man's elbow until the old man lets go. He springs free and turns to him, red-faced, his small chest heaving.

The old man sits on the barrel of the cow, her ribs bending beneath him. Throws up his hands. He swings his legs away from the child, leans. Then swings them back again.

The old man rises. Draws a cow skull from the briars, the vines tittering after it. Angled bone, gaping mouth in a soundless bawl, its eye-holes searching with their absence. Puts it in front of his own face in mock show. Sees the child through its curves and the child remains expressionless, unmoving. The old man tries to fit it over his own head but it does not fit.

He's about to pitch it into the weeds but the dour face of the child, glaring at him, glaring. He grabs the child again and forces the skull over him with one hand. Pressing down until the edge of bone scrapes over his flesh. Slips into place.

The old man steps back. Jesus, he says.

The teeth of the skull bared. The rat-chewed knitting of bone across the back.

He reaches for the child again but the child backs away. Come on now, the old man says. Don't be daft.

He reaches for the skull but the child will not come to him.

The old man stands in the dusk, among the bones of the animals he has failed. He takes the neck strap from his pocket and wrings it over his knuckles, the slick rot rubbing onto his skin. Lets it dangle and then bunches it again. He kicks away a leg bone. Says, sure then.

The old man and the child in the Ford. The empty chain wrapped around the back hitch, dragging along the lane. The tractor moving easily without the weight, the road clear before them. The old man stares ahead, keeps the tractor straight. The skull turned towards him. Watching him.

THe
PUB

The old man walks behind the child. Hands on his thin shoulders. The child wilting beneath them. As if they were to guide the child, but the child, he knows, would not be steered by him nor by anyone. The hurl tucked under his arm. The brightness of the day fades behind them as the old man waits for the shapes of the pub, the Clarke Martin, to settle out of the dim light. Dull brass railing over the counter stretches across the room like a fault line. The half-filled bottles lined against the wall reflect a smoky image of the bar. The old man lifts his hand to the corner of the room, not looking. Three hands lift in return.

Malachy stands behind the taps. Points at the Guinness until the old man nods, then pours. The glass drifting as he stares at the child, stout flowing over his hand. Malachy says, sorry about that now. Sorry. His cheeks reddening. Wipes the bottom of the glass, then his fingers. Throws his towel over his shoulders again and keeps his head down.

Gill leans back and says, you fuck. Go take mass from a guitar-playing priest. By the way you're moving you can't tell me farming isn't killing you.

The old man sips. Licks his lips. Never promised it wouldn't, he says.

Lonegan gives a knowing look to Gill, then drifts into nodding absently. Farrar clutches his pint, stares out the window. The three of them men who had once farmed.

The old man grabs the child with both hands and pulls him onto his lap. The child twists and writhes, his arms outstretched to the scratched floor. Like hauling a tin sheet in the wind. Pushes against the old man until the old man lets go. The child wears the trousers of the old man, the waist tucked over. The neck of the geansaí stretched to fit over the skull.

Gill rips a beer mat in two and then folds his arms. The top of his knit cap, black, crumpled on his head. There's talk of putting condoms in schools. Free for the taking and all.

A proddy thing to do, isn't it? Lonegan says.

Condoms, Farrar says. Condoms, condoms. He turns towards his beer. Slouches and scowls. Then turns back towards the window.

The old man's hurl lays across his knees. His jeans still dark from the clay of the field. Being without a johnny hardly slowed any of ye, he says. He looks them over and then says, in the day.

Gill throws his arms. A performance for the others. As he always does in front of the old man. The queerest and oldest standout, you'd make for a mighty installation at the city museum. He looks to Farrar for support, but Farrar only glowers. His hand tucked in the front collar of his shirt, elbow drooping over his stomach. Sure maybe an art show, Gill says. Throws his arms up again.

The child remains in the dull-cast light of the window. As one apart. Weather-picked bone, top-heavy over a thin chest. Like the wet leg of a calf emerging from a bawling heifer, the old man thinks. The start of something more to come, even if he couldn't say how. The child watches the other men, but they do not meet his stare.

The walls of the Clarke Martin lean. At times the floor creaks even if those inside are still, the building shifting beneath them. Old scythes and rake tines and spade handles hang from the rafters. Sometimes they turn over the heads of those drinking, although no lorry has driven by and there is no breeze anyone could feel. If asked Malachy would say they always have, they always have. With these twisting artefacts there is movement always at the edge of a patron's vision, or just out of sight.

Malachy closes the dishwasher behind the bar, sets it to wash. Strange times indeed, he says. Today there was hail. On this island, sure? At this time?

The men at the table palm their glasses, trace the watermarks of their beer. Rub their hands unconsciously over their thighs.

There is a bench against the wall, and on it instruments. Banjo, guitar, fiddle. Sometimes a patron slumped in the corner would suddenly rise, play an old tune to the empty seats and vacant bar, then return to his stool, his head dropping again. The instruments never set on the floor. Never cased and latched.

Lonegan stands and turns away from the table. Opposite the child. His head large and bald, a thin rim of hair over the ears. Puts his hand behind his back, which pulls apart his tweed jacket like the opening of curtains. You see Sligo nearly took it from Mayo? Just fell one short under the bar.

You don't give a damn about the Gah, the old man says.

The Gah, Farrar says. The Gah, the Gah.

Mary Flaherty is meant to come by, Lonegan says. Will you ask her of news from London, Íosac?

The old man stares into the table. Turns the head of his hurl in his lap. The scars on his knuckles fade, reappear as it rotates.

Mary Flaherty will drop off her extra tomatoes, Lonegan says. Good woman, she.

I'm not sending him away, the old man says.

Gill, his hands in front of him. His knee bumps the table, pushes foam over the top of the pint glasses. Do you drink coffee because she did?

She had been to London.

And you wouldn't follow her back.

The old man looks at the child. Motions for him to come closer. The child stares back. With eyes like stones at the bottom of a stream bed.

It's not for our sake, Íosac, Lonegan says. We're for the boy, see. Hell, he says, and then says, we know what he means to you.

The old man holds his hurl upright against the floor. Has no intention of getting up. Just wants to keep pressure against something around him. I'm his keeper, for Christ's sake, he says.

It's not natural, Farrar says.

Jesus, Farrar, whispers Gill. Íosac, we're not saying it's not natural.

He's not natural, Farrar says.

The old man holds Farrar with a hard eye to see if he will look in the direction of the child. Lonegan steps in, stands between them. Places a hand on the old man's shoulder.

You'll end up dead, Gill says.

I won't be dead, the old man says.

You'll be dead.

Then I'll be dead.

Malachy pours a lemonade from behind the bar. He puts a cherry in it. Places it before the child and then slides it closer with the back of his hand. He wrings the towel he holds. The child takes him in with the full weight of his eyes. Malachy reddens again. Steps back and busies himself drying glasses.

Has he another place to go? Lonegan asks. The question echoes in the murky light.

THE HEADLANDS

The old man's hurl falls away. Lands in the clay soundless. He bends behind the stone and leans into it. Its oblong shape toppling the furrow. He lowers himself again, pushes it over again. Gathers himself, bends and pushes again. The stone leaves a winding tunnel over the soil on its path towards the hedgerow. The Ford 2110 heaves to itself. Pulsing sound spreading over the ploughed ground. Always, the old man thinks, that pulsing sound. The silhouette of the child in the tractor cab. A pool of shadows in lesser shadows. He stares ahead, his details lost behind the glass.

The old man jolts. He looks up. He once thought the sky was made of paper, but now he knows it's stone. A rook had been crossing the sky, sinks lower, lower on its course as if pressed down from above, bending away into a far hedge.

The child stands on the tractor steps. Small hands clutch the handle, pale, nearly translucent. The skull gazing vacantly to the hill line. The old man does not know if the child sees things that he does not. But the old man feels them.

A dog appears on the headlands.

It did not emerge from the hedgerow. Did not come trotting down the winding road. It manifested itself instead at the boundary, where the worked ground met the shared tract. Head bent low. The black hair on its neck lurches as it steps onto the old man's land. Lips pulled back, baring its teeth.

The dog thrashes forward. The old man runs.

A hailstone cuts through the air. Bounces off the tractor's bonnet, falls to the soil. The child stands by the turning motor. High over the empty field. The dog and the old man come upon him in opposite directions.

The old man swings his arms, pulses. Each breath a glancing ricochet in his chest. His work boots sink into the clay every step, the ground itself pulling him in. He reaches down without slowing, picks up the hurl, tilting over a furrow and nearly falls from his momentum.

The black dog's shoulders throb. Its flesh ripples over its bones. It races towards the tractor, tearing the land beneath it. Eyes narrowed and focused on the child, unflinching, unyielding. It collapses the distance between them as its paws kick up billowing dust. Wet fur slick, arched.

The child watches it approach.

Clay grips the work boots of the old man. His footprints grow deeper behind him.

The dog nears the tractor.

You will not! shouts the old man.

The dog leaps at the child. The old man brings the hurl down on its head. Having not the strength to stop the old man crashes into the wheel of the tractor, his body thrown into the tyre rubber, steel housing. The dog bellows. Skids below the undercarriage.

The old man lies on his back, still clutching the hurl. The engine of the Ford rattling over him. He stabs the hurl into the soil, hauls himself up, slowly. Pain shimmering through his joints like the wind-rattle of shed windows. Both hands shaking.

The dog circles to the front of the tractor. Its coat matted with clay. Like it has risen from the ground itself, growling at the old man.

The old man holds the hurl towards it. Not today you won't. Not today. He pokes at the animal. The dog feigns at him.

Snaps. I don't care, the old man says. He prods the air. Takes another step forward. I don't care.

Then swings the hurl wildly about him.

I don't care.

Ice cuts through the air and burrows into the heaved ground, leaving the earth pocked and dented. It pushes into the furrows, its impact resounding with grainy clatter. The colours of the field and its rocks and stray weeds bleach away behind the plunging hail. The hedgerows teeter, the brush shaking violently and the leaves tearing apart and falling beneath them. Moisture beads on the arms of the old man and melts on his skin, the sudden coolness heightening the ache swelling inside his body. The boot prints the old man made across the soil fill in and disappear. The air around him is heavy and loud, and he cannot tell where the dog went because the valley around him has been curtained from view. The ploughed and unploughed ground merge together in the wet haze, and the tractor pales into silhouette. The horizon has collapsed around them. Only the shape of the skull remains visible in the torrent, the hail recoiling off it. The child's eyes unmoving inside the echoing bone.

THE
STANDOFF

The door catches, jangles. Young John Allen enters the Clarke Martin.

He saunters, stops suddenly when he sees the old man, the child. Shakes his head. Turns to the counter. Geir Sullivan, his cousin, follows. Geir stands in front of Young John and surveys the room with his thumbs in his belt loop, round shoulders slumping.

Young John's face collects gullies of shadows as it frowns. He wears a John Deere hat that makes him look boyish at first until the features of an adult settle out. He folds his arms and rocks on his feet, and then stops himself from fidgeting by sitting down. He shrugs, though unclear whether to dismiss the old man or the circumstances that brought them together.

The child stands at the end of the bar. His faint breath pushing from the shadows beneath the bone. His face a pale reflection in dark water. Holds a full glass of lemonade in front of him. Unmoving.

Some weather, Young John says. Raises his voice but does not look in the direction of the other men.

Hail, even, Geir Sullivan says, though it is clear he is not being addressed.

How they milking? Young John asks.

They're milking, the old man says.

He is called Young John because his father was also John

Allen. His father a hard man to do business with because he would not shake hands until he had the better deal. Everyone could see Young John's father waiting for his old man to pass so he could use the insurance to buy the Moran place next to him. The grandfather seemed to know and persisted stubbornly. The ruins of a shed that would not fall. But eventually John Allen would have his way.

The old man rests his hands in his lap. Veins run over them like a dark net about to rip open. His three friends with their arms crossed.

Malachy wipes the counter in front of the taps and drops two beer mats. When no immediate order is given he backs up and stands in the doorway of a supply room, grabbing the top of the frame, tipping forward. His bare stomach beneath the end of his shirt. A radio plays quietly from the clutter behind him.

You're looking a bit worse for wear, Geir Sullivan says to the old man.

Gill leans back. Shapes a pistol with his fingers. Cocks it and fires at Geir.

Geir flinches.

The old man looks to the child but does not call for him. The hurl across his knees. Places one hand on the shaft. The old man's shoulders are still, rigid. Lifts each foot to square it beneath him.

It's not that I don't admire your determination, says Young John Allen.

You have no idea, the old man says.

Or stubbornness.

Keep swinging your lad in my face sure I'll bite it off, the old man says.

Gill closes one eye and fires his pistol again at Geir Sullivan.

Young John Allen asks Malachy for a Guinness. Malachy looks between him, the old man, the child. Leans towards the tap until the rest of him follows. Young John's own father died a few years ago. Aneurism and leaving no insurance money behind. The town waited to see how much of his father's tenets Young John would follow. He took out a loan and bought the Smyth place, even though the Smyths had no intention to sell that anybody knew of. Seemed to be answer enough in some people's mind. A fitting snapping into place.

Sad, Young John says, colour rising on his neck. Sad when the lorry passes by without stopping.

Lonegan stands over his own table. Flips it over.

Jesus, Patrick! Malachy shouts.

Its hard edge bounces off the floor. One of the glasses shatters in a wash of stout. Others roll in circles in front of it. The men sitting there jump to their feet. Gill already taking stiff strides towards the bar. Farrar kicks a vase rolling on the ground. Scatters plastic flowers against the wall.

The cousins stand. Malachy lunges forward and grabs the end of their shirts from the bar, telling them to be steady, be steady.

The old man's face grows red, turning vivid the white stubble on his neck. Coarse skin on his arms ripples as he clutches the hurl. Tight as he can.

You think I'm the bad guy, is it? Young John says. Straining forward. The back of his shirt tented out. Am I going to be the bad guy? Am I then?

Entitled twats, the lot of you! Farrar shouts. Twats, he yells. Half-turns in each direction, and then again yells, twats!

Take a swing, ye Old Shits, Geir says. Get on with it then!

The old man leans on his hurl with one hand and with the other thrusts his finger towards Young John. It shakes in the air between them. With my last, he says.

The child approaches Young John Allen. Those in the pub still, let their arms drop to their sides. Young John glances at the old man, and then to the child. Settles into the child's gaze. Malachy lets go of his shirt. The fabric falls against the waist like the sealing of an envelope. The old man keeps a squinted eye on the window, at the world outside, as if anything was liable to come from it. The child reaches out his arms and Young John recoils. Then leans forward, peering. You want me to lift you? he asks. The three patrons still breathe loudly. Look around them, uneasily, like the building might fall to rubble. Young John takes an unsteady step forward.

The child is thrust backwards by the flat of the hurl on his chest. He stumbles. Pushed behind the old man. The old man turns, holding the narrow end at the face of Young John Allen.

Not as I live.

Young John Allen looks past the roughened wood before his nose. His gaze slides along the shaft, past the old man holding it, to the child. The old man sees the child staring at Young John, the child's head tilting. The old man winces.

The door creaks open. The old man lurches forward. Hurl raised.

It cuts a path through the air and then comes to a rigid stop. Mary Flaherty gasps. Drops her basket of tomatoes. They roll under stools and along the wall. She cowers under the raised shaft.

The old man grabs the child and leads him out of the Clarke Martin, placing a hand on Mary Flaherty's shoulder as he pushes by. She recoils. Watches the two of them disappear.

THE
VISIT

The grey saloon pulls off the lane. Slips into the tractor ruts of the driveway, jostled in the mud-rimmed track. There are only two kinds of people who drive that fast in this part of the country, the old man knows, and they are the young and the white collared. Both with a tendency to race between stone fences like blood from an artery. The music inside muffled by the windscreen. Glass that casts the interior in silhouette. A man emerges, arches his back, grabs the front of his belt.

The old man slaps the bonnet and turns towards the shed. Paul, he says, as he walks away.

Íosac.

Paul O'Grady's grey suit blends into the sky behind him. The bank's logo on it. Tucks a clipboard under his arm, but there is no sign of a pen the old man can see. The old man walks through a puddle, scattering water over the gravel. O'Grady steps around it. They stop at the heifer shed first.

The old man puts one foot on the gate of the pen, leans on it. Your mother, she well? Recently weaned calves suck on his pant legs, butt their polls against his shins. Their tails swing wildly behind them. Frenzied by want.

Well enough I'd say.

I must get down and call on her.

She keeps busy enough, I'd say.

The old man's best bale of second cutting in the hay ring at

15

the front of the pen. A waste to feed good hay to heifers. The old man wonders if O'Grady remembers enough of his own upbringing to notice it.

Some weather.

The old man says, some weather.

They cross the farmyard. The old man feels the eyes of the child on him. The child watches the two men from the pulled curtains of the sitting room, his knees on the couch. The child does not have to be told that he cannot come out.

The old man had carried out the broken gates, the used tyres. Behind the hedge that ran along the property. Content at first, shifting some of the rusting clutter of the farm to the tall grass, but soon dragged out the empty teat-dip barrels and bale wrapping. He imagined his farm in the eyes of another. Then took out the worn plough parts, buckets of stripped nuts and broken engines cleared from the corners until he had extinguished himself into an early sleep. The bones of the shed, piled and bared to the darkening sky.

Prices have been low, that's not surprising, the old man says. Clearing his throat. But we've kept on. Always have.

Good on you there.

We've never been pretty men in our family, but hard ones to kill.

The old man looks back, but finds no response from O'Grady. He opens the door of the dairy and walks through it first. The air heavy and damp. The pull of heat across the room as the bulk tank cools the milk from the inside. Paul O'Grady stands in the centre of the wet concrete, the floor channelled with the veins of wash water that had run over it across the years on its path towards the drain. Arms crossed, he is careful not to get close to any wall, objects that can rub against his shirt, leave a stain. He is middle-aged and balding. Holds himself with reserve.

The old man pulls out a five-gallon bucket and sits on it, his head bent and then lowers still. Half-heartedly knocks his fist against the steel of the tank. The room fills with a hollow echo. Tests at three-nine fat, three-eight protein, he says. Somatic cell under a hundred and fifty thousand always. You don't get that with the big guys.

That's very good, O'Grady says.

You'll want to see the cubicles and the parlour. They're in order, all in all. The old man holds the door open for him.

A bit lonely, I'd imagine, O'Grady says. I know you have the boy, but.

They walk the alley, the heads of cattle drawn in unison to follow them as they pass. A few of them rise to their feet, hooves clacking off the grooves in the concrete. A calico cat trots across the end of the shed with the carcass of her half-eaten young in her mouth. The flesh bright, coddled in her teeth.

The old man grabs a handful of baleage in front of the bunks. O'Grady feigns towards it in mock examination, nods. The old man casts it in front of him. It rains on the concrete, soundless.

The banker lifts his hand, shapes the farm to a simple gesture. Bet you're looking forward to the day when you take a break from all this.

The old man's dusting of lime on the cubicles, the alleyway, pulls a chalky drift into the air. Clings to the bottom of his wellies. Cows rock their heads as they chew their cuds, their jaws turning. Dazing to stare down the white plane and see them all at once.

The old man takes another grain bucket hanging on a nail, turns it over. He slowly lowers himself on top of it without the help of the hurl. Puts his head in his hands.

O'Grady winces. Looks away.

You would give a loan to take another man's place, but not a loan to the first man to keep it?

The country, she's different now. It's not my call to make.

You went to London for a few years.

It's not that I went to London, Íosac. O'Grady pulls his clipboard to his chest. Standing over the old man.

The old man nods. A simple act to carry him into oblivion.

You're a good man, Íosac. At least I think so.

The bank. You like it there?

It's an easy life.

It is, the old man says. Raises himself from the bucket and walks away.

THE
ROOKS

Every milker hangs below a cow. Rubber grasping, throbbing, kneading. The old man returns to the steps and sits, his stained knees splayed in front of him. The child walks along the pit, reaches his hand to touch a flank or press the back of his knuckles against an udder. Sometimes he drifts among them in the holding area as they wait to be milked. They reach towards him with leathery tongues, tug on his shirt. Follow after him. Feral cats lay in the dusty angles of the building, tucked into the loose chaff. As natural for the child to be in the shed as for the old man to milk twice a day.

The silhouettes of rooks shift behind the cloudy glass windows. They beat their heads on the panes, a dissonant note against the pulsation of the vacuum pump. The child spreads his fingers over the muzzle of a cow. The animal lowers its head, nudges into him. The first few years after the child came to him the old man had looked for ways to lift the curse. Bad luck, he thought, that was sure to pass. Something that would right itself in the natural balance of things.

The old man props the door of the parlour so he can hear a milker kicked off. Takes a shovel, runs it along the feed bunks. Cows lifting their heads, shaking them, scattering saliva. The shovel collects the long stalks, refuse of the silage. The old man gathers it at the end of the bunk and then takes a bucket off a nail and forces the silage in with his wellie. The child waits at the end of the shed. The old man clears one bunk, then the next. He will bed the heifers with it later.

The old man stops, stills the child. Rooks clatter above them. Collecting on the roof, calling angrily. The child looks up, then to the old man.

When the buckets are full and spilling the old man takes one and walks past the sick pen. The cows do not stir as he pushes on their foreheads and tells them to be well. The smell of iodine rises from the teat dip stains in his clothes. An acidic taste on the tongue, one he is used to, but in turn thinks that maybe hell tastes like that too. If hell tastes. He looks back to where he was just standing, where the child has remained. The rocking whispers of the milkers fill the space between them. A ceaseless pulsation flooding the alley.

The bucket in one hand. The hurl in the other. He touches the child on the shoulder as he passes, leaving loose stalks on his shirt. His weight shifts side to side, walking the length of the shed. The child follows behind him, scuffing the chaff with his wellies. The curse as much the child as the skin he was born in. The silence a part of him. The way he was made, the old man thinks.

The old man lifts the door at the front of the shed. It draws back on its track, groans, then reveals the horizon at dusk. Rooks whirl above them, shrieking. Their wings cut through the air, rendering a static beneath their screams. Their circling draws more in from the landscape. Others rise from distant hedgerows. The funnel grows tighter in the air, a slurry of black feather. The child huddles by the old man's legs and grabs a fold in his jeans.

The old man stands silent. Gazes past the birds in front of him. Does not wave his hurl at them nor shout at the turning sky. One rook plunges towards the child and the child steps back. A second bird thrusts itself in front of the child's face and spreads its quivering wings. The child stumbles. Falls.

The birds sink in closer around the child. Instead of carrying him back to the shed the old man pulls him to his feet and bends before him on one knee.

Listen to me now, he says. We are born of this ground. Let it tear itself from our feet before men take it from us. We do not move. We do not yield.

The old man picks up the child and carries him through the driveway. The rooks screech and dart at their faces. He lifts his hurl to clear the path before them.

We do not yield, he yells.

THE
ANNUAL

Hop! Hop! Hop! Hop! Yells Conor the clerk, stomping feet, salutes the band. He turns the Quinn girl, dips her shoulders, sends her away. She spins and twirls, grabs her dress, taken by O'Sullivan. He winks and weaves her through the crowd amidst the spinning bodies. The instruments twitch in time and music spreads over the town dancing, dancing, and a pint tips over and everyone shouts. The light is bright and slick along the veneer of the walls like a membrane stretched over them all, them turning, curling. Spin, dip, twist, clap the Quinn girl is sent across the middle with her dress flowing above her thighs until The Buff grabs her fingers and swivels her around. Mulgannon came, sure enough, she says, before she's slung into the centre, where Conor the clerk grabs her by the waist and takes her back.

The old man sits at the end of a table, his chin in his hand. The chairs around him empty. The child stands to the side, facing the dance. The old man has put a clean white T-shirt on the child and given him his better pair of shoes, stuffed with packing paper from the last time he butchered a cow. The skull does not sway to the music nor nod in rhythm. The old man slaps his own lap, but the child does not move. Instead, the child turns to the priest, who stares at him from the other end of the table.

The priest leans forward on his elbows, crouched. Both hands on the base of his pint. His head large, hairless. His nose angular like a shattered field stone. The black cloth bunches over his stomach. His eyes dart around him, deeply set beneath his forehead. Looking away from the child. Looking at him again.

Tap it, tap it, turn and square. The school teacher puts her hands on her hips and bobs in a sprawling reel on the hardwood floor. Flings her hair and whoops and the others move back, whistling and shouting and elbowing each other. Is it out of spite, then, that he brings the boy? Shouldn't we be taking cover? says another, and laughs, and glances behind. Yip-yip! Slide and shift and tuck and spin, toe-tap, toe-tap, tap. Hands in the air as they turn. A sheen runs along the floor from the beer that slips over the edge of the glasses as they swing through the air. Jesus Christ Jesus, him and the priest both. Some pair they are. Have you been to his mass, the reek of brimstone. Have you been? Don't suppose anyone has. The school teacher is raised in the air and carried around the outside of the floor, grazing the fingers that reach towards her. The accordion wheezing. The banjo player lifts his head to anyone that acknowledges him.

The Annual occurs in the lodge. Candles burning in cloudy glasses on the table. On the wall an altered sign that reads No Poking, the cigarette turned phallic. The priest gazes at the child, twisting his head. The old man leans forward to intercept his gaze and pull it onto himself.

Good to see you out, Mulgannon, the priest says.

Watching out for the flock tonight, Priest?

You brought some company yourself I see, he says, nodding at the child.

The whorish head on you, the old man says.

The musicians swing their elbows in time, fiddle, flute, guitar, a pulse passing between them. The townspeople slap their thighs and tip their heads back laughing, the pale of their necks bared to the rafters. Who knows what's in his head? Who knows what he will do? The priest or the farmer? Jesus! The smoke of cigarettes twist from the limp hands of men talking along the walls and in the tight seal of pressed lips of those stomping wide-eyed, the smoke curling around their thrashing faces and spreading over them like netting. Binding them all. Roaring faces and knees and their sides appear and recede into the haze, grabbing at each other and bellowing, tongues protruding in feverish cheer. An arm emerges from the fog and reaches for the child as it spins by, and another hand grabs the sleeve and pulls it back in.

The old man scrapes the end of the hurl back and forth against the wooden floor. He motions with his head for the child to come closer, but the child will not. The old man turns to the priest.

Is the end still upon us, Priest?

Fuck yourself, Mulgannon.

Your frock is heavy with sulphur.

And the cowshit on you.

The old man leans back, chuckles. The two of us.

The skull turns his head to follow the townspeople that pass. The face beneath it shadowed by the glare of the light. If an inebriated voice calls out to him he does not answer it.

Will there be signs with the end times, Priest?

You cunt.

I'm asking.

Your theology is manky and mangled as your own self, Mulgannon.

Isn't all of ours, so?

The priest takes a sip of his pint, sets it down. Wipes the moisture off the table with the flat of his hand. There will be signs, he says.

The music thins away as the players let the instruments settle to their laps. Only the banjo yet sounds, the player plucking with his eyes closed and swinging his head until a hand reaches over to still him. The townspeople have slowed in their turning, bumping into each other, untangling themselves. Some step back, tuck themselves behind someone else. The colour and gaiety gone from their faces.

What is he doing? the clerk asks.

The child stands on the dance floor. He blows gently, his small cheeks lifted against the inside of the bone. His hand sways in the air, slowly, bending the wrist. The floor clouded with the weathering of shoe soles in the empty space between him and the bystanders. He looks into the centre of the crowd and where his gaze falls they back further. His hand waving. Blowing. He swings the skull around and a shiver passes among them.

Take him away, Murphy says from the front.

Mulgannon leans back in his chair, chin in his palm. Does not meet the pleading glances.

Get him out of here, Johnston shouts.

God, what is he doing?

Some feign towards the door, but do not want to be singled out.

Be decent, will you Mulgannon?

The child blows and waves his hand. The air rushing over the flat broad teeth. The end of his trousers puddled over his shoes.

The priest stands. His chair scraping on its legs, nearly tipping. He walks onto the dance floor.

That's not a boy, he says. He half-turns to the right, left. Lifts his palms up. Soul-stealing péist walk among us. The hour of the end draws near, the priest says, the top of his shoes slapping against the wood.

The eyes of the town follow him. Some nod their heads unconsciously.

The priest stops beneath an old painting of the town's centre. Its frame with dust in the ridges. The crowd stands, huddled, folds their arms, grimaces. Times of trial and turmoil come, the priest says. He faces the child, but backs into the townspeople. They make room, absorb him. And that is not a boy, he yells, his arm shooting forward. That is not a boy! Mulgannon, take him away!

The old man lifts his head from his palm. Sips from his pint. Sets it down again. The priest's finger still pointed at him, directing everyone's gaze. The old man runs the back of his hand across his mouth, and then his shirt. Lifts his glass again. Finishes it. The face of the hurl rasps on the ground as he draws himself up.

He picks up the child, puts him on his shoulders. The child's leg swings towards the priest as he is lifted. The priest recoils.

The old man and the child walk into the night, the child swaying above the farmer.

PLAYING

The child stands, slack, holding a hurl in one hand. The shaft leaning away from him.

Here we are, the old man says. He stands a few metres away, holds the sliotar before the child. Turning it over before him. The old man swings and hits it in the air.

It lifts up, over the horizon. The skull does not move. The ball hits the child in the chest, rolls off him. Towards the old man.

The calves in the hutches around them stretch their heads out of the openings, straining over their buckets. They call out and squirm, their knees pressed against the front boards. Cattle in the cubicles are restless, pace the alley, their hooves scraping against the concrete. One Friesian rubs her chin along the gate, the gate flexing on its hinges. A pigeon alights from the front of the shed and absorbs into the sky around it.

The old man picks up the ball and walks back. Come on now, he says, tapping his wellies. Come on, sure. He holds up the ball and hits it again.

It strikes the child on the skull, tilts it. Bleached-white bone over his pallid flesh. Its open eyes cast up. The sliotar drops to his feet. The head of the hurl still on the ground.

The calves thrash their heads, bellow. They reach out with their tongues towards the emptiness in front of them.

CONVERSATION WITH LONEGAN

Lonegan stands over the old man, face heaving white. I don't know how to be anything.

The old man leans against the slope of the bank, his arms folded against his chest. The silhouette of his body pressed into the sedge grass. His rod lies next to him, prone and still. When he casts the float the line falls silently over the water. The last of the sun gone, leaving pink and blue fluorescence in its wake.

Lonegan shifts on his feet, says, since I don't milk cows. I still get up at five in the morning, because something tells me to. Don't know what it is, but it's there.

The sky is reflected on the water. A plastic sheen over the darkness beneath. The shadows of small trout flicker near the edge. The old man looks at Lonegan and then at the country before them. The lake is at the top of the crest, a patchwork of hedgerows and stone fences beyond it. The floats rest past their wellies. Beyond that the edge of the world.

I should have brought the child, the old man says.

He's fine.

You're sorted now, Patrick. More than you ever were.

I know.

The old man looks over his shoulder behind him, as if he can see the child miles away in the house.

The bus will soon not stop here. Is that true? the old

man asks.

He picks up his rod, reels the line in a few turns, and then sets it down again. The filament stretches taut and then slackens, the bait resettling. Lonegan still standing in front him.

Ah Jesus, Íosac. How's Mary Flaherty going to get her medicine?

Sit down Patrick. You're souring my view.

Lonegan kicks at the grass. Says, think of it. First the barracks, now this. Next the bank will pack up and take the cash machine with it. We'll have nothing but our thumbs to stick up our arse. He digs his toe into the earth behind him. You have a fish, he says.

The old man's float twitches a few times, crumpling the image of the bright clouds in front of them. The old man picks up the rod, holds it out. A thin tendril in his rough hands. The red plastic takes a heavy plummet, jolting under the surface. The old man jerks back. He feels the weight of the unseen thing resist him and he turns the reel over. A silver flash of the fish's body, shocking the surface. It dives deeper. An instant of light against the black water, never taking its full shape. And then the tension is gone.

The problem is, you know, Lonegan says. What have I to whinge about now?

The old man reels in the line. It glints in the last light of the day, hangs flaccid off the tip. The float remains in the water, turning about. Thrashing.

That's manky enough, the old man says. Rubs the frayed end of the filament between his fingers. Should I jump in and get it you think?

Lonegan pushes his hands out in front of him. I'll buy you cod and chips at McHenry's.

Would I have to listen to you there? He sets the rod down. I should have brought the child.

The float disappears again. Rings echoing in its place, spreading to the edges. Moments later, it emerges further along the shore, bouncing on the water. The creature writhing, concealed below the surface. Its struggle conveyed by the piece of red plastic in front of the men.

It's killing you, Íosac. We all see that. The thing is, not having it will kill you too. The others don't know, but Jesus I do. I do. Lonegan picks up his rod but is too agitated to reel it in. Drops it back in the sedge. Not that I'm telling you something you don't already know.

The old man taps the side of Lonegan's knee with the rod, trying to get him to move. The sky grows deeper purple, fading into blue at the horizon.

It's the lack of struggle.

Jesus, Patrick.

Will you listen to me? Lonegan opens his palm. Holds it in front of him like something heavy and strange. He slaps himself in the face.

Patrick. Not again.

Lonegan's face is pulsing, condensed. Bulging eyes, unfocused. Standing over the old man like a swaying tower.

You know yourself, Íosac. Lonegan hits himself again. You know yourself and that's why you still do it. Farm, he says, and strikes himself.

The old man tries to push back, away from Lonegan. The slope of the bank presses against him. Holds him there.

Hit me, Lonegan says. Nodding at the rod.

Patrick.

Íosac, I need to feel it. Pick it up.

You're on a mad day.

Pick it up.

The old man holds the rod. Loose filament curls in the breeze.

This is farming, Lonegan says.

Patrick.

The shapes of the men in the water before them, pale and thinned, their features stretched to distortion. Circled by the clouds that float on the water. The old man pulls himself to his feet. Watches Lonegan, the horizon. The rod at his side, moving with his breathing. The manure of his wellies mixed with the smell of water.

Lonegan reaches for the rod.

The old man jerks back. Turns around and snaps the rod. Takes the thin part and snaps it again.

The red float sits atop the water, still. In the middle of the lake and from that distance impossible to know if yet anchored by anything.

The old man pitches the bundle into the sedge. God damn we're fools, he says, and walks away.

THE PHOTOGRAPH

The old man ploughs, digs the lime pile field, keeps the shares turning. Stares at the line in the soil before the bonnet of the tractor, the border of the worked ground and fallow land and keeps the front tyre on it. Knows he hasn't blinked because his eyes hurt. Making straight furrows because that is a mark of a good farmer, although maybe he has just decided that. Reaches the headlands, lifts the plough. Starts down the other end.

A handful of rooks follow the shares. Bound along the overturned soil, poking at the worms and insects that scurry. Crowd over each other like children. The clay tossed behind the machine, the machine rattling. The undercarriage of the field unrolled.

The top of the cab lined with felt, the felt pinned by fencing wire, still drooping down. The old man reaches into its loose fold and pulls out a photograph. Its edges frayed and backing worn to the feel of leather. Of a girl. Runs his thumb over it again and slips it into the felt.

The old man strikes the brakes. It rocks him forward and then back in the seat. His limbs still vibrate though the machine is stilled. Takes a heavy breath and pushes it out of him, stirring the dust before his face. Then turns.

An island of upright grass that the ploughs have missed. Tear-shaped, with the dark colours of untilled growth.

The old man lifts the plough, turns into the unploughed ground. Breaks a channel into the spring weeds. Shares bouncing over the field, swing around, around. Until the old man pulls the Ford, the plough, into where they have just been and drops them into the soil.

The rooks settle after the equipment. The old man stares at the front left tyre, doesn't turn away from it. Doesn't look in the mirror at the spot he missed to see it overturned. He reaches into the felt again, takes out the picture. Lets it drop out of the window.

The old man tries to judge by the sky if it will rain, but he knows the sky is not a mistress to follow. Runs his fingers over the dials to clean them of dust, check on the insides of the machine. Watches the tyre turn. He closes the window and opens it again and then stops the tractor.

He leaps off the steps and hurries behind the shares. He kicks at the ground with the front of his wellie, kicks. Pushes through the furrows of soil until her face is unearthed. Plucks the photograph away.

He settles in the seat again, puts the Ford into gear. Rubs the picture on his knee and puts it back into the felt fold of the ceiling.

RETURNING

The old man loosens the chain to the cowshed gate. His leather gloves stiff, clumsy. 202 lifts her head and bellows, anxious to join the herd again. The saliva around her mouth green with the soft grass from the graveyard. The child straddling her withers, straight-backed, absorbing her movement as she shifts on her front hooves. Other cows crowd along the bunk. Sometimes lift their heads to call back to her before stretching to pull at the forage in front of them.

The old man knots the lead around the post. Raises his hands to take the child. The child leans away. The old man reaches for the child but the child swings his small fists and strikes him. 202 bellows again.

The old man lets his elbows rest on the back of the cow, reclines on her. Feels the letters from the church sign in his back pocket and only now remembers that he took them when he left, although he is not sure why. He sighs, taps his knuckles against her ribs. A yellow feral cat turns the corner of the shed, stops when she sees them. Then puts her head down, slinks along the tractor ruts.

The old man rolls off the cow and faces the child. Were we going to let him away with The Annual? he says.

He reaches for the child but the child leans back.

The old man turns and scoops up the cat in one hand as it passes. Strokes it forcefully under the rough leather, its skin pulled tight from its eyes, mouth. The cat tries to bend out of the old man's arms but he presses it tighter against him as he runs his palm along it. Finally tosses it behind him.

Sure then, the old man says. He stands in front of 202 and pulls the halter from her head. Throws it over his shoulder. The old man pushes the gate open. It pulses on its hinges, slowly swings wide. Creaks. He steps out of the way.

The animal hurries to the bunk, her head bobbing up and down. Thrusts herself between other cows as she reaches for the silage. The child high atop her. Above the backs of the other Friesians that collect along the alleyway.

We have found someone to stand against, the old man shouts to the child. Then wraps the chain around the gate. Latches it.

THE BOG

The old man turns off the boreen, into the bog. The trailer creaking as it lowers and raises itself out of the ditch. Smoke from the exhaust pipe settles around the cab. Joins the low sky. The child, sitting on the arm rest, grabs the lip of the window as the machine rocks back and forth. Keeps his knees pressed against the side of the cab to make sure they don't touch the knees of the old man. A five-gallon bucket swings on the tractor's hitch, filled with unopened letters.

Rows of stacked turf spread between the hedgerows. Each piece leans against another, drying. The old man sets the Ford in the lowest gear, turns the throttle down. The child moves into the driver's seat when the old man jumps off. The tractor creeps forward, the steel trailer following behind it. The child stares ahead. Doesn't blink. Each bundle sits on the soft ground in loose construction, in danger of collapsing in the old man's hands as he bends over them. He grabs the bottom two pieces, hunches, slowly raising it all up high enough to toss into the bed. It scatters in the air.

Without the hurl the old man heaves along the row, does not allow himself to groan as he bends down. He collects the turf for the town, dumping it into their common shed for them to distribute among themselves. It is extra work, but he is a man that works. That's what he means to say in doing it. Or that he's decent, in the count of things. The old man moves along, tractor-steady. Passing through the souls that wander the bog. In the trailer the bones of the land. The pulsing of the engine echoes a rhythm his body can tune itself to. The bog underneath him gently shakes beneath the crawling machine. He cannot blame the child for jarring the world when the world itself is already unstable.

The old man allows one turf stack to remain. A cairn on vacant ground. Offering to the spectres that might tread the cut land when he leaves.

The child does not look at the old man as the old man climbs into the driver's seat, shuts the door. Motions for the child to drive but the child doesn't respond. The old man pushes a grease gun away from the clutch with the side of his foot, then bends, puts it beneath the armrest. The Ford creeps into the boreen, swings. Raises in pitch as it heads towards town.

The old man turns on the radio and sings and nudges the child with his elbow. Jerks the steering wheel left and right in time with the music and sends them both rocking in unison. Lifts the bucket up and down quickly. Says, come on now.

The old man takes the corner sharply, for effect, the trailer pivoting on the hitch. Yeehaw, he says. Pokes the child's leg. Then the old man slows and turns down the radio. His neighbour, Colm the Pipe, walks the road. The old man gives Colm the Pipe a wide berth. Lifts his finger off the steering wheel. Colm the Pipe watches the tractor as it passes, the bucket of envelopes that sways on the back.

The old man puts his forehead against the front window and looks to the sky and then to the turf in the trailer, pulls on the throttle. As good on the way there as back, he says, grabbing the parking brake.

The old man slips the five-gallon bucket off the hitch, pushes through the hedgerow along the boreen. Comes upon a small patch of waste ground with trees rising thin and gangly between brush. Walks to the burn pile beneath a stand of alders, fringed with dry cinders. Stands over a dead heifer, mouth gaping, half-submerged in used dairy wipes, bale wrapping, parts of the shed broken and aged. Her burial and ceremony. The old man cannot ask her if this is how she wants it to be, so on the heifer's behalf he believes it so. Takes a can of diesel from the crotch of a tree and scatters it over her.

The old man retrieves a few bricks of turf, throws them into the pile to help it burn. Dumps the unopened envelopes over the stack. The old man has never opened the post. Letters can say all manners of things, but he has known them only to harm. They slide off the heap, pile over it. The logos of feed companies, banks, and solicitors. The old man tips over the bucket. Sits on it and pulls a half-chewed cigar out of his back pocket and sticks it in his mouth. A matchhead flickers. He lights the corner of an envelope that sticks out of the pile, leans back as the invoices twist and writhe before fading away into embers over the turf.

The child sits in the tractor cab, staring into the distance.

IN THE
CHURCH

The old man wears his leather gloves, holds the rope lead slack in his hand. The cow follows behind him. The animal's head heaving, the yellow plastic tag reading 202 swinging from the cartilage hole. Hooves click off the paved lane. The child sits atop the cow, his back straight. Thin knees clenching her pin bones. The old man lifts the shovel to him and the child balances it across his lap. His small frame sways in line with the old beast as they pass between the stone walls. The bare skull over the cow's head, lurching with it.

Too heavy to be carried to town anymore the old man had asked for Nancy Rourke's jennet for the child. The animal bucked and jerked so violently under the child that the old man could hardly set him on before the creature was twisting in the mud. It brayed from the pasture day, night afterwards. Echoing through the valley. So incessant the bawling that Nancy Rourke eventually sent it to the barracks in another village to be shot.

The cow does not hurry, nor change her ambling gait with the child. She went dry several years ago and hasn't caught with the bull since, but this use has kept her around. Her switch swings slowly, heavily. Sometimes the long bristles snag in the briars that reach over the walls, but she keeps walking without slowing, her tail pulling free and shattering leaves behind her. The stones dark and heavy with lichen. The tops have weathered, sometimes crumble into the lane. The old man would stop and pitch it into the brush. Then continue again, the steady click of the hooves marking their passing once more.

They walk by a neighbour's sheep paddock, the animals leaning over the stone walls, staring to the east. Their attention held by something unseen on the vacant landscape. A daft animal, the sheep, the old man thinks. Fine for some but not a man like himself. A man could not make his stand for sheep.

The rustle of an old Renault engine carries on the breeze long before the vehicle turns onto the lane. Jimmy Haskins behind the steering wheel, the mop of his hair no higher than the dashboard. Although he cannot be seen, the Colonel, his grandfather, lying in the backseat. Jimmy, twelve, takes his grandfather home from the Clarke Martin every Wednesday. So Jimmy isn't tired for school, Malachy locks the doors at night with the Colonel still slouched in the corner, head hanging down. Jimmy has to wait for lunch break at the Sacred Heart. The old man pulls the cow against the wall and waves as the car creeps forward. Jimmy lifts a finger off the steering wheel, doesn't take his attention off the road.

The old man and the child cross the bridge, over the twisting whispers of the river below it, marking that they are entering the town, leaving the hinterland. The cow lifts her tail and arches her back. The child hands the old man the shovel and leans forward to balance himself. The old man scrapes the manure off the tarmac in one motion, leaving its wet shape behind. Tosses it into the river. It falls with a dark plunk. The old man looks to the child for a smile, and the child smiles.

The child high upon the cow as they walk past the cafe, the flower shop, the betting office. A few shoppers behind the glass of SuperValu turn their heads to follow their passing. Some on the street cross to the other side, entering the road with their faces still turned towards the old man, the child. The old man lifts his hurl as a greeting. Usually the old man ties the cow to the stop sign at the edge of the town. Today he does not.

A crowd has collected around the open doors of the church, the church usually quiet and unattended, especially the middle of the week. The cow follows behind the old man. They weave their way through the markers of the graveyard. Past a stone cross that leans, weathered. The cow leaves prints in the grass that lift away behind it but don't entirely disappear. They stop at a stone wall that separates the burial grounds from the churchyard. The cow pulls at the grass on the other side, chews wetly.

One by one those gathered turn towards them, and when they do they flinch or draw back. The crowd shifting and sighing, a door half off its hinge. Looking over the cow, the child. Some cross themselves. They cannot turn away from the child, from the skeletal bone on his face, cannot put it into words. So they turn to the old man. Standing with his hands on his hips.

The priest steps from the crowd. What cuntish thing?

The priest spits out a half-smoked cigarette. It topples through the air like a twig off a tree. He crushes it under his boots. Hooked-nose, eye-bold. Shaved head like the brass of the Angelus bell. A large man made larger when he straightens his shoulders to speak.

What bollox? says the priest. Then says, Íosac Mulgannon that animal desecrates on the holy property ... and fuck please, the boy.

The old man runs his hand along the neck of the cow. Leans on it.

The cow laps at the grass from mounded soil, the grave marker beside it. Lifts its head as its jaw turns. The child tips forward. Prone. Palms pressed on either side of the animal's withers. The skull looks at the priest. Tilts towards him.

The priest swallows and crosses his arms.

They took the chalice, shouts Naughton. He stands in the

back. Unable to keep the news he had.

And the baptismal font says Walsh the Pile.

And the collection plates, says the priest. Be gone, Mulgannon.

The old man walks the cow along the wall. Towards the gate. The heart of the town, stolen away, the old man says.

Sure, it must have been the travellers on the Pat Kelly Road, Burke replies. Unaware of the old man's mocking tone.

We've never had trouble with the travellers before, Naughton says.

It's a gang of them Dublin boys come down. Sure they came down to feed off the fat of the land, Colwell says.

The East will take everything from us, bit by bit, the lorry driver says. May it be damned.

All stand silently as the old man pulls the cow into the churchyard. The child on top.

The crowd parts before the beast. They behold the child with fixed gaze, for they know the child and the things attributed to him. The child, the child, they had whispered in their homes, the heavy curse that sits upon him. What claim had he to bring the disruption he did, to pull at the corners and take from them the comfort of order. Although they are still, something inside of them leans away. It is that the world does not love the child and if he passes too close and they are not strong then they might not be loved too.

And please, the boy what? the old man calls out. Slams his hurl on the concrete.

The priest steps before the front of the building. Scowling. As he comes to rest the cloth settles and his shape retracts.

I can't decide how you were going to end that sentence, the old man says.

The cow, lurching, climbs the steps. The child grabs the animal's neck. The people fall in behind it, at a distance.

The priest backpedals. Tries to stay ahead of them.

The old man says, I'm sure the church doesn't put lies on its signs. That being the gospel, I'd say we're very welcomed.

The priest clenches his fists. Breathes deeply, the air rushing from his nose. He looks back and forth between the townspeople, the crucified figure on the front wall. At the bulge of himself. Ready to topple.

The old man takes the shovel from the child and sets it against the wall of the church. The dark smell of manure rises from its blade. The old man grabs the child with both hands, lowers him to the ground. Cups the skull in his glove. The lead rope hangs loosely from the cow's jaw, is drawn across the stone floor. The old man takes the child by the hand. Walks towards the priest.

The priest spreads his legs, refolds his arms. Head titled and lips pulled back. The old man and the child approach and his eyes swell, his head shaking. Stop, he yells, his finger in the air. This is a house of God.

The child grabs the old man's hand tighter and looks up at him.

But the boy, the priest says.

If he is not the child of God then God created nix, the old man says.

But the world, it turns against him. I've seen it myself!

The world will turn from us all.

The child starts to pull back but the old man drags him forward. Both hands on his small arms. The weathered gloves leave stains on the child's skin. Who decides what is natural? the old man asks.

The priest backs up until he finds himself against the wall.

The old man picks up the child and jerks him towards the priest. The priest presses back against the wall. His hands out. The child flails and stretches his arms out to the old man's chest, but the old man holds him in the air and shakes him at the priest. The skull sliding over his eyes.

The priest crouches to the floor, shielding himself. The old man thrusts the child at him again.

RЄADING

The old man hunches against the backboard, reaches for the book off the dresser. The child lays flat on the pillow next to him in the bed. The old man leans on hessian sacks stuffed into each other. The hurl on the floor beside him. Making a straight, thin shadow. The book is worn, edge-frayed. The smell of old feed drifts over them.

The hound sprang. Cúchulainn tossed the ball aside and the stick with it and tackled the hound with his two hands. He clutched the hound's throat-apple in one hand and grasped its back with the other. He smashed it against the nearest pillar and its limbs leaped from their sockets. According to another version he threw his ball into its mouth and so tore its entrails out.

The top of the dresser is cluttered with sheared bolts, stripped nuts. Cotter pins emptied from the old man's pockets over the years. His milking clothes crumpled on the hardwood, blue paper towels sticking out of the back pocket. The child lays fully clothed, the skull gaping at the ceiling. Headlight beams roll across the bare walls in front of them. Two searching eyes, glowing.

The old man stops, watches them. Looks down at his hurl. Then keeps reading.

A cow bellows from the cubicles, a call pulsing in the darkness.

THE PTO SHAFT

A metallic clunk and at first the old man thinks it's a rock glancing off the rota-spreader. When he turns around there is no hutch manure, wet straw flung from the machine. Shear pin, he says to himself, because he is alone. Stops the tractor, the Power Take-Off. The Ford quiets to a rocking drawl. He slips on his geansaí. It is not cold but the air feels sharp after stepping out of the cab.

How many shear pins has he fixed, how many spreaders has he outlived. Folly, he knows, to think, but. The tops of weeds brush along his trousers, flicker behind him. And he thinks of this, of having no more broken things to patch, to shove on yet another day, and yet to have fought and pushed to that day and to have no one taken those days before it. Until his time can be over. What will be the final count of broken things in the end, and the pleasure of no more. He rummages through the tool box.

His knees are sore, burning and cracking from sitting. He hobbles with the hurl. Swaying left and right like rye in the wind. Steps between the Ford, the spreader, in the narrow space between them. Leans over the PTO shaft. Sings, God damn shear pin, stick it in Mary Lynn. God damn shear pin, will probably stuff her again.

The shaft starts spinning.

The old man yanked down with great force, bent over the

knob of the hurl. Pulled downward, downward. The end of his geansaí and then t-shirt wrapped around the PTO, stilling it in place but it twitches, jerking, dragging the old man down into its mechanics to be coiled and flung onto the grass.

The old man wedges his hand between the end of the hurl, his ribcage, forces a grasp on it. Shaking, quivering. His breath sputtering through his clasped teeth. Glances up once. The child stands by the front tyre. The skull merging into the grey sky. Tries to yell at him to lift the lever up but the shaft pulls on him more. Every joint, bone in the old man stacked erratically inside him and another bit forward and he will crumble and wrap around the PTO and be thinned away. He does not try again, does not look up.

The old man takes a mouthful of exhaust settling around him, turns it inside him, and roars. Pushes against the hurl, pushes, bellows, his back lifting, the flannel over his shoulders stretching, holding, tamping his frame until it finally tears with a howl and the old man falls backwards to the fallow ground, his papery skin bare among the flaking goldenrod.

The old man lays on the unploughed land. Pain rushing to connect the parts of his body. His mind numb, nothing. His shrunken frame among the weeds, like something cast aside. His hand slowly pushing along the earth, the only part of him moving.

When he feels his hurl he drags it to him and then gets to his knees, slowly. Pulls himself up on the hurl. And then stands.

The old man stands, swaying but not falling, as his two shirts flap rapidly around the spinning shaft. The child nowhere to be seen.

Try harder, he yells to the open field.

THE BUS
LEAVES

The old man opens the door to the shop. Allows the child to enter first, the child clutching a sack that smells of cattle grain. The bells by the hinge rattle above them.

Bread, bacon and a packet of McVities, is it? the shopkeeper asks. You know where they are. He leans over the betting section of the paper, his glasses on the bridge of his nose. Ears curling on a pin cushion face. Circles a few listed odds and turns the page. Took the chalice, took the font. They can have me next so. Would you buy a Playboy if I had one?

The old man palms a loaf of sliced bread and keeps it at his side. I'd read it in the jacks before putting it back.

Internet is so shite around here, wondered if there might still be a call for them.

Wooden shelves, grey dust on the ends. Dark stains pooled on the floor. Cardboard boxes stacked in the corner. The scent of aging fruit heavy in the air.

The old man puts the groceries on the counter. Lays a handful of coins down and leans back on the hurl. The child holds the bag open. The top bunched in his hands.

Don't need to tell you how much it is. Same as it was last week, as it always was. It'll cost you the same next week as well. The shopkeeper bends down towards the child, taps the back of the skull with his pen. Was he really bitten when he was found or is that hearsay?

The skull turns towards him. Silent. The shopkeeper grunts and scratches another mark on the paper.

You two boys make a lot of people nervous, the shopkeeper says. They think they want to like you, but they don't know what to do with you. I told them hell now, world is still turning, with us or without us, won't make no difference. Things always changing, don't matter what we think. We might as well eat bread, bacon and McVities. The shopkeeper raises an invisible glass to toast them and then looks at his watch.

Jaysus, he says. Come on, come on. He rises and then shoves the old man and child out the door, forcing them outside. Almost time, he says. He gestures until the three of them are in the street, the groceries and coins still on the counter.

A crowd gathers before the Clarke Martin. They fill the width of the footpath, spill into the parking area, all of them silent and staring at the concrete. Children, sensing the heaviness around them, remain quiet. Clasp the trouser legs of their parents. Couples with their arms around each other. Gill, Farrar, and Lonegan stand in front. Shake their heads.

The red and white bus crests the knoll outside of town and heaves along the dotted line. The eyes of the town follow its coming, its slow turn onto the street they stand on. Watch it ease to a halt in front of them. A swell of gas released from its undercarriage. Onlookers steady themselves as if they can be blown back by it. The door opens.

Malachy comes out of the Clarke Martin with a half-empty bottle of Powers and hands it to Connolly, standing next to the door. Connolly unscrews the cap, takes a swig, and passes it to Finnegan's wife. She swallows, wipes her mouth. Surrenders it. The bottle moves through the crowd as the bus shakes on its tyres in front of them. Exhaust whorling into the air. The image of the driver hidden behind the windscreen and the steps of the open door leading only to uncertain shadows.

Mary Flaherty emerges from the crowd. Places a feeble hand on the railing and pulls herself up the steps. Her flowered purse swings loosely from her elbow. The doors close behind her and she disappears behind the sheen of the glass. She is replaced by the reflection of the people, small and distorted, huddled together.

How is she going to get home? someone whispers, but there is no reply.

The bus pulls away. Signals, eases into the road. Gill grabs his belt in both hands, lowers his head. Robinson sits against the front of the Clarke Martin, legs splayed on the footpath. Some rock foot to foot, slowly. Like weeds risen through the concrete, pulled by the wind. The pocked cheeks of aging men folding and refolding as they chew on the insides of their cheeks, spit. Old women closing their eyes.

The bus leaves the town. They watch it drift towards the east. Gill heaves the bottle of whiskey at the back window. It glances off the corner of the vehicle and falls to the ditchgrass unbroken. The men closest to the bottle remain still for a moment, out of respect, and then retrieve it. They pass it around again as the bus tops the hill and disappears from view.

THE OLD MAN PLOUGHS

The windscreen of the Ford vibrates. The world seen through the dusty glass shakes violently, the things that built it upright now unhinged by his small tractor. The old man drags the mouldboard plough behind him, scraping it over the earth. He works the west field under a sky the bottom of a counterweight. He's not alone in the valley.

Young John Allen and his men in the east field. They disk and lime and seed the field, their band of equipment circling. Their machines roam the land, quelling it beneath them, roaring to be heard. Twenty acres in the name of Nancy Rourke stand at rest, separating that of the old man, of Young John. Mule-grazing scrub, a thin buffer between men.

It was Paul Moran that owned beside Rourke before Allen. Moran drank, but he worked. In the way of things as the old man knew it, that made him a good man. If Moran's plough broke the old man went over, because the field had to be ploughed. The way Allen's cultivator takes the corners of the plot in high gear it means to wear away the imprint of Moran on his fields.

The soil turns slowly behind the old man. The ground behind the plough is dark, but as the sky takes back its moisture the soil turns pale at the ends of the field. Syringes, ear tags, ankle tape emerge from the heaved land as the machine passes over. All once in the grates of the shed and cast out by the rota-spreader. Rusting bolts sloughed from other machines. A coulter from the old plough. Slouched hide of a cow. A spanner sticks from the ground behind him that he had lost last season but he does not stop for it.

At times the Ford of the old man and the disk of Allen pass by Rourke's in parallel. Once the old man pulled his sleeve to his hand, dusted off the window with his forearm. Not to see them better, but to make it clear he was not looking at them. During these times the bay of their engines bled through the glass of the Ford's cab and discoloured the sounds that the old man knew to be his working machine. He keeps the ploughs steady.

The men in Allen's field take a break, pass flasks, biscuits. The old man will not stop. Piss from the steps once, maybe, and swing his piss over the tyre. But will not stop until the field has been ploughed. He ploughs not just to complete the act in the day, but to feel the day push against him in hours that ache his body and pull at his mind. To know that he still can. To know that he will always.

The old man stares not at the wheels but in front of the wheels to keep the tractor straight. Corn spurrey twists from the ground like nerve endings. The front tyres roll through tillage weeds, the weeds slick and broken before disappearing under the cab. The skull from a premature calf rises from the ground. Barren eye bones. Watches the tractor pass. The air is thick, dusty inside the cab. The old man breathes deeply and loudly through his nose, but the sound weaves into the drafts pulling around him. Loud clattering and jostling. It shakes at his wits, at the shuddering ligaments that root thought—renders the mind from the body, memories and desires, man from idea, man from land. He sways inside himself.

A field is a lifetime. So it is by natural law that when the headlands are reached a man who gives himself fully would not be measured as he was on the first furrow. But I plough still, the old man thinks. Voices echo around him.

His consciousness. The radio. Six hours of ploughing is six decades of farming, is that there is no way to tell what said things are in his mind, outside it. The tractor is his mind, the ground his body. He slaps himself. What daft things a man becomes when in a tractor cab for so long. He raises the front mouldboard over a large rock and saves it from being broken, from having to stop. He looks ahead, keeps it straight. Looks behind. The vibration of the machine saddles his thinking. The land behind the dusty windshield is of two kinds, ploughed and unploughed. The old man ploughs.

I plough I plough, the old man says, I plough across this stony earth. The sun does not set in a sunless sky and so it is to man himself to know what he has done and to know his soul. The ground cleaves before him. I plough I plough, he tells the clutch, he tells the gears. Pain rings through his shoulders, looking behind him as he must, a glinting current, an internal melody. He breathes in dust and vibrates in his seat. When they break him in two they'll find he has no bones, no blood. That he is a dust-packed shell, hardened and hollow. The soil turns behind him. I plough I plough, he tells the grease gun in the corner. To the end of the field. He bounces in the seat. Is shook, jostles. The vulgar ground. If all ground was honey it would not ache so to plough it. Honey, he yells at the dashboard. He raises the front mouldboard and lowers it again setting it back to task, to peeling away the skin of the world to reveal the scowling bones beneath. He strips the field of the fallow grass one furrow at a time. Each pass leaves four rows of heaped resolve, compass straight, the next pass four more. The field a letter to the world. He knows the violence of the land of the heaving tractor because he knows the violence inside himself. Him shaking in the seat, body turned to nothing is him tussling with the open field before him and being numbed and being lifted. Lifted up, above the seat, above the valley plane, so that he is a man between land and sky, belonging to neither, a transition, a flicker of an image of a man. I plough I plough, the old man says.

The tractor seizes. The old man rocks into the steering wheel and back to the seat.

The old man has pushed the brakes. It is because Young John Allen stands before him. One foot on the ploughed ground, one foot on the unbroken land. A punch-drunk smile, John Deere hat halfway over his eyes. Something in his hand. Jesus Christ, the old man thinks. What has he in his hand?

The old man descends the steps carefully, holding the grab bar like a child clutching the dress of its mother. His knees shake, balance staggers. On the ground he is no more sure-footed. He wobbles over the clay.

Young John steps towards him with his hand out. We'll take the weather while we get it, he says.

The old man does not shake his hand.

Young John steps back, falls into picking at the dirt under his finger nails. Glances up at the old man, then to the ground. Looks like it's working up sound enough. Here, see, brought you this sandwich. Figured you'd be out fitting today.

Young John holds out the sandwich wrapped in foil.

The old man stands wild-eyed and shining. Half-turned to the other farmer. His chest heaves. His body red. Pulsing.

He slaps the sandwich away.

Young John Allen, with empty hands, sticks them in his belt loops. He shifts on one foot. Then the other. Jesus Christ, he says. Then walks away.

The Ford roars as the old man pushes the throttle and sets it in motion. The shares rattle behind him like pendants colliding on his chest. The silhouette of the old man is bent, pitched forward. The mouldboards throwing the ground in front of themselves. Clay washes over the wrapped sandwich and takes it from sight.

BEATS HER

The old man stands over 202. Her body sags in the grass. Tail-limp and pooled. Her eyes greycast, the sky inside them. The skin pulled taut over her bones in a great tension she is not released from. Her mouth gaping, stupid.

The old man hits her.

He lifts the flat of the hurl and swings through the air and strikes her in the face.

You whore.

He steps and smashes the top of her head with the wood. A damp echo. Pries the hurl under her chin, lifts her face. Lets it fall to the ground.

You mighty bitch.

He kicks her. The top of his wellies flap against his trousers. Steps on her and then off her. Picks up the hurl again and drives it into her ribs. Says, I was going to go. Bought the ticket. Swings his fist into her neck. You bitch you bitch you bitch.

The child stands behind him.

THE MIDGES

The old man lays on his back in the tormentil. Its tendrils curl around him. The moisture from the bog creeps into the fabric of his geansai, casts a coolness over his skin. Next to his head sits a stack of drying turf. A small altar. At the top an unopened envelope wedged upright, the back facing him.

The child to the side, his motions flitting in the old man's peripheral. The child stands on the edge of the cut ground. Over the dark bog water, fetid and rancid. The skull the only part of him light enough to be reflected in it, its thin shape floating at his feet. The child plucks at the midges that land on him. Pitches broken turf into the murky pool and watches it splash around him.

The letter is above the old man, the old man on the ground, looking up to it. Sharp edges against a sallow sky. As if hinged there. The words inside knitted into each other. Still undeclared. He reaches behind him with a lighter, lights it. It writhes and twists. Falls to ash over the ground. The flash of heat spreads over his face. Fills up his chest. He stands up.

They're coming, Child. They're coming. I don't know if I'm strong enough.

The old man walks the bog. His wellies pushing through the sedge. The ground recoils from the impact of his steps and lifts after him. A body of midges drift through him. A shifting apparition bending over the bog grass. Brushes along his skin.

Shapes around him and disappears.

He runs a hand along his arm and continues. Used to be man was left to confer with the ground he stood on. He took from it and it took from him. Now they went and made it hard to be what a man was. They didn't have to, I believe that Child. But they did.

The ash of the envelope lies curled under the bricks of turf. The old man reaches his foot in and crushes it. Dissolves it into the bog. His wellie print under the stack.

If comes a point that you're the last one standing then that's who you measure yourself against.

The old man straightens. He limps to the cut ground. Staggers as he moves.

The shape of the child stands erect on the bank. In his place glimmers static. The edges drifting. Midges cover his body, a thick, fibrous matt that lay over the relief of his features. The skull above it, clean. Its angles cavernous. They draw in to him from the landscape, pulled into the shimmering film. He does not move, does not stir. The twitching of their wings bend small whispers around him. The bog speaking to itself.

The old man holds up his fingers, shaking. Runs them along the child's wrist.

A streak of pale skin. Quickly covered over.

The old man takes the child in his arms. His hands sink into the whirring flesh. The child a bone inside it. The old man stands on the bank of the cut bog, the water. Lowers himself. He steps into it, slips. Falls against the sliding soil.

The old man stands waist-high in the russet water. Holding the child.

He lowers him. Arms trembling. The child disappears. Dark water collapses in his wake. The old man lifts him again.

The water sheds off the wings of the insects. They hold fast. Glistening. The old man, half below the ground, looks to the sky, to the child. Grasping the child's flickering silhouette.

He lowers him again, strains to hold him there. The child's

nose above the surface. The child's eyes watching him inside the skull. Glowing in the murk.

Small blemishes appear on the surface of the water. The flat wings of the midges that float up.

THE OLD MAN AND THE BEAST

The old man sets the milkers to wash, drops his coffee cup into the basin, trudges into the daylight. Beaded dew on the grass. Watery sun on the hill. There was corn in the bottom of his mug this morning, as some mornings there is. Manure splatter. He stopped grieving it one day and then another day stopped dumping it out. Sometimes he keeps it in his bottom lip. Running the cracked kernels along his teeth. As he does today.

Does not like to go to the post box at the end of his driveway but he goes there anyhow. Does not sort through the invoices but wads the bundle in his back pocket, the paper cringing. Slams the box shut. Looks down the road. Jolts.

A black figure emerges beneath the glare. It stops, heaving. Barely fits the width of the stone walls. Thrashes its head. Smoke rolling from its nose.

It calls out.

Which of the king's warriors are you? the old man whispers.

The beast lurches down the lane.

The old man takes his hurl and goes to meet it.

Its feet echo in the daylight, the bulk of it rippling as it moves. Eyes broad and seeking. Swings its head back and forth, lifting it into the air and sending a deep, pulsing roar between the stones.

It stops before the old man. Snorting.

The old man stands with his hand over his eyes. Spits corn at his feet. It bounces over the road, skittles away. Then he raises the hurl. Braces himself.

Voices lift behind the beast. The sound of breathless shouting. Running. Only when the words are repeated do they start to take shape. The creature sidesteps and kicks out and looks behind it.

Stand clear, Mulgannon, for fuck's sake. Young John Allen rushes upon them, wellies slapping against his trousers. He stops ten metres before the animal, not wanting to spook it further. That bull's a mean head of cac, Mulgannon, he says, leaning back with his hands on his hips, panting. Just let him through. He'll tear you apart.

Geir Sullivan and a few men working for Young John come running down the lane. Young John puts his hands up to slow them. Points at the bull.

The trailer door swung open on the way to the mart, Young John says. Wiping his face with the front of his shirt. Sending him in since he's such a hard boyo, nasty as hell. Think now I'll just call the guards to put him down.

The bull swings its back legs. Mucous dripping from its nose ring. Shimmering in the sun.

Are you afraid of him? the old man asks. I'm not. He raises the hurl higher.

Geir and the two hired hands collect behind Young John Allen. Trying to gather their breath enough to chuckle, laugh.

You'll get killed, Mulgannon. Let him pass. We'll ring the guards, Young John says.

He will not pass.

Jesus, if he's mad enough sure, Geir Sullivan says.

What's the point of it, Mulgannon? says Young John.

The bull brays and butts the stone wall and sends mucous against the stone.

Can I have him then? If I get him can I have him so?

Young John shakes his head. Jesus, he's all yours. Then

catching himself says, I mean, listen Mulgannon. Young John bends his hat brim in his hand.

A car slows to a stop behind the men. Singleton and Lally get out. They slap the door shut. The sound sends an electric pulse through the bull and it kicks its legs in the air and throws its backend to the side. It leaps towards the space between the old man and the wall and the old man shouts No! and steps in the way with the hurl raised. The bull rams his head into him and pushes him back, but the old man does not fall. The bull turns and jerks towards the other men in the lane. They scatter and whoop. Climb onto the walls. The car in the road halts the bull and the bull turns towards the old man.

The men stand above the old man, the bull. Cursing. Motioning the old man up.

Don't put your blood on my hands, Young John shouts. He looks to the other men. Says, Jesus.

Mulgannon finally found someone as stubborn as him, Geir Sullivan says, but no one laughs.

The bull lurches again and the old man yells Heya! and snaps the hurl against its head. The beast startles, wrenches back. Its chest throbbing as it stares wide-eyed at the old man.

Will you stop? Will you stop please? Singleton shouts. He is a small man with glasses. Bites on his thumb. Turns to Lally. I don't understand why he does this?

He's mad as fuck is why, Geir says.

We know you're tough, Young John says. There, I said it. Is that what you wanted to hear? You're a tough son of a bitch and harder than us all.

Stone shards flake to the road as the men shift on their feet. The shadows they cast in the low light stretch across the lane.

Please Mulgannon, Young John says.

The bull thrusts to pass Mulgannon, tail raised and when Mulgannon steps in his way the bull sinks his skull into the old man's stomach. The old man folds around it and lifts in the air.

The bull carries him backwards but as he jerks his neck to

shed him the old man grabs the nose ring as he falls. The hurl skids away. The beast bellows as he drags the old man over the ground, the animal's head tucked back. The old man's shirt bunches under his arms and his skin tears against the hard surface. He hits a lip in the road and plants his foot against it and swings the creature in an arc, its shoulders crashing against the walls.

The men above them shout and wave their arms as the old man keeps his feet moving to stay upright and clutches two fingers over the thin metal while the beast thrashes. As the bull nears the gate to the old man's driveway the old man throws his weight into the cornerstone and is pressed against its edge as the bull swings through it, bawling.

The bull on a dead run to the shed. The old man dragged with it, his eyes closed.

CONVERSATION WITH GILL

The old man comes upon him with his back turned, slouching. The square slants of stone he sits on feathered by grass on the edges. The cut rock in the blue water a pile of angles. The unused quarry. The horizon burns red above them.

Going to ask me why? Gill says.

The old man bends down on one knee. Leans on it.

Gorse blossoms around the edge of the cliff, bold yellow flowers. The sky bleeds over the flat stone.

Gill pulls at the grass. First few years I thought I'd get so mauling bolloxed some nights I couldn't milk cows the next day if I had them to milk. By fuck.

The old man stares at his back. Lifts himself. Then sits down on the same stone. There are better ways of not farming, he says.

Say that to your reflection.

The old man grunts.

Gill throws a stone. Shatters the blue calm beneath him. Everything that came after was about finding something mad to belly up to. Jesus, when you say it out loud.

You'd need a guitar-playing priest for those sins, the old man says.

Anything I could do that I couldn't if I had taken the farm, by fuck.

Gill and the old man stare at the hole in front of them.

The bottom of their wellies reflected back. Their breath, their fidgeting the only movements on a landscape of colour and rock. Their elbows touching through the fabric.

Gill throws another stone. Ever did acid?

I couldn't.

Fuck your mother, that's what I'm telling you.

Their bodies cast no shadows under a sunless sky, but absorb the red tint until they glow at the edges.

You going to be able to make it back? the old man asks.

Women too. Times I didn't like fucking them I fucked them all the same. When the drink wore off and I lost the shine. If it felt like work all the better.

The depth of the water beneath them signalled by the darkness of blue it holds. The deepest part below the two men. No way of knowing how far down it goes. The things that lay on the bottom.

You're always so fecking quiet.

You're nervous, the old man says. Ever drugged before?

You didn't ask me why I'm doing it. Suppose I told you though.

The old man pushes off his knee. Lifts himself.

Just wanted you to stop by, Gill says. See if I had any bad reactions right away, and so.

The old man steps around the edges of the rock. Past a bush of purple heather. A stillfire of hue. He turns to Gill.

They haven't made a place for men like us yet.

They haven't made something for us to do, Gill says.

The old man walks away. Leaves Gill on a rock, waiting.

THE SICK PEN

The old man stares at the backend of a cow, his elbows in his hands. The cow lays still, breathes slowly.

Behind them Geir Sullivan jerks open the shed door, squeezes himself through sideways. Stands there with his thumbs tucked in his belt loops. Hey there, he yells out. Rocks on his heels. Yells out again and then walks through the shed.

The Great Mulgannon, Geir Sullivan says, coming upon the old man. Stands next to him and folds his arms. Then says, Christ Almighty.

A red mass protrudes out of the back of the cow, bulges in the straw. Leathery caruncles drying, stiffening in the murky light. Her uterus spilled out behind her.

Listen, says Geir Sullivan. He wears a hat that says Cusack Feeds. Takes it off and puts it back on again. I'm sure you're willing as I am to let bygones be bygones and all that. He looks the old man over. Then shifts on his feet and holds out an open palm.

The old man walks away.

Geir Sullivan stares after him. Turns to the cow. Then follows the old man.

The old man enters the dairy, takes a calf bucket. Pumps the lever of a plastic barrel and splashes teat dip into the bucket. Fills it with warm water. Yellow bubbles swell on the surface and then burst. Geir Sullivan trails the old man out the door.

The old man climbs into the sick pen again. Swings his leg over the highest bar and sets the bucket down. It tilts in the bedding. The old man picks up a come-along from the corner of the pen and drags it to the down cow. Tosses the rope towards the rafter stretching over them. 202 lays in the far end of the pen, watching the old man, the other cow. Flicks her tail at flies on her topline. On the third try the old man tosses the rope over the plank, connects it back to the pulley.

I just been hired, see, by Cusack, Geir Sullivan says. Sure, it's alright. I'm to enquire after accounts and all that. Mostly the overdue ones. Jesus, what's going on here, he says, nodding at the cow.

The old man slips the hip lifters over her pins and turns an old bolt shaft until it grips her bones tightly. Straightens himself, exhales. Starts working the crank, raising the backend of the cow.

Geir Sullivan says, anyway, they sent me here. In fact, I'm the only one that would come. Others say it's futile, or well. Just don't feel comfortable or something. But I said hell, I'll come.

The cow scrapes at the concrete with her front hooves but doesn't have the strength to lift herself. Resigns to being on her front knees. Her backend slowly turning as the rope twists.

The old man pushes up his sleeves. They bunch at his elbows. Dips his hand into the bucket, lathers. The dark water clinging to the hair on his arms. Says, the dead pile will take you. Maybe not today though.

The old man carefully rubs the rough tissue. Lifts the bucket to his chest and pours it, the warm liquid following wiry paths over the organ, his fingers. Falls to the hay. The cow jerks, dust filtering down from where the rope flinches on the wooden rafter.

The old man steadies himself behind the cow. Gets two hands beneath the bulbous pile and then puts his shoulder under it. Shakes as he lifts up. Slips it back into the cow, pushing it into the caverns inside her. Then he stands there, his arm inside the cow. Tells Geir Sullivan to come here.

Geir Sullivan clutches at his beltloops and kicks at the chaff in front of him. Turns to stare at the shed walls. The old man says it again and Geir Sullivan finally steps forward.

Run your hand along my arm, the old man says. Until you find my fingers. Hold her in place for me.

Surely will not, Geir Sullivan says. This isn't my job.

The old man looks him over. Says, probably never been inside a woman either.

Geir Sullivan chews on the inside of his cheek. Shakes his head. Jesus Christ, he says.

Geir Sullivan pushes his hand through the vulva of the cow, his arm sliding against the slick skin of the old man. Leans in until his fingers reach the tissue lining. The old man pats Geir Sullivan's hand inside the uterus of the cow before freeing himself.

I'm going to need to leave here with a payment, Geir Sullivan says. Marching orders, you know. I'm sure you understand.

The old man takes a steak knife out of the back of his pocket and tosses it into the bucket. Tips the bucket and swirls around the little bit of teat dip still inside. Bends and unlaces one of his work shoes, pulling at the dirty string as it becomes longer, clumps of mud breaking apart as he forces it through the eyelets. Drops the shoelace into the bucket.

The old man grabs the fold of the vulva and needles the end of the knife into it. He clenches the shoelace in his mouth, the bitter taste pooling around his teeth. The string stretching half his length and swaying. The internal fluids of the cow cool on the old man's arm. When the knife pierces through the tissue of the vulva the old man slides the knife into his back pocket again, pokes the end of the lace through the hole. Pulls. The cow lifting her head and straining from the lifters.

The old man spreads the vulva flat between his fingers and takes the knife again. Geir squints. Leans away from the old man. 202 rocks forward at the other end of the pen, finally pulls herself to her knees and gets her hindlegs beneath her, rises. Her loin dipping as she stretches, puts her head over the gate. The old man's wrinkled fingers numbly work the flesh, the shoelaces. He stops sometimes to curse and wipe his forehead on the end of his shirt.

Eventually the string weaves around the outside of the vulva, both ends falling over the back of the udder.

Take your hand out, the old man says. But do it slowly.

As soon as Geir is clear from the end of the cow the old man ties the shoelace into a bow. Well, he says. Then says, there you have it. You're an alright assistant, Sullivan.

Geir Sullivan shakes his arm out. Didn't expect to be doing vet work today. But damn.

The smell of iodine rises off the clothes of the two men, the top of their collars damp with sweat. The old man bends down to rub his hand on a dry patch of straw. Then steps over the top bar of the gate and takes a syringe, bottle, off a nearby window ledge.

Now comes the uncomfortable part, says Geir. I'm afraid I'm going to have to ask for that payment. It would be helping me out.

I won't, the old man says. He fills the syringe and gives the cow a shot of penicillin in the neck.

Geir Sullivan crosses his arms. Looks to the cow and then back to the old man. Tilts his head. You won't, Geir says. That's not a great stroke on your part.

The old man levers the crank, slowly lowering the cow. When her weight settles in the bedding and the rope slackens the old man slips the lifters off. He pushes her rear legs beneath her to make it easier for her to stand later.

The old man looks up. Sees Geir Sullivan still staring at him. Says, can't get water from a stone, and so on.

Fucksake, you're a pain in the hole.

The old man sets the knife, syringe, and bottle into the bucket. Grabs the lip of the bucket and heads towards the dairy.

They'll put a lien on this place, if they haven't already, Geir says. Banks and lawyers and all of it.

Geir Sullivan grabs the old man's shoulder as he passes.

The old man spins around. Lifts a finger at him. I've given more than enough for what I have. Try to take more and see what happens.

The old man takes the knife out of the bucket, grips it. Turns back to the dairy.

I will, Geir Sullivan yells at the old man. He pounds his fist on the gate, making the latch rattle. Glares at the old man's back. I will!

BY THE RIVER

The child rocks slowly on the withers of 202, the beast's head rising and falling as she follows the footpath, hooves echoing between buildings. The child clutches a hessian sack in front of him. Inside is bacon, bread, and biscuits. The Independent. A shovel lays across his lap. The lead held loosely by the old man's hand.

The cow stops, hunches. The old man balls the front of the child's shirt in his fist, holds him on the cow, keeps him from falling. The shit splatters on the legs of a bench. When the cow is done he pulls her ahead, her tail still pointing out as her frame resettles. The old man takes the shovel, lifts it behind her but does not use it. Gives it back to the child. He picks up the lead again. It'll take to the sewer soon enough, he says, not looking back.

They leave the town and cross the bridge and the old man leads the cow down a path. Through the briars below the bridge. The dark river turning. At the bank the old man wraps the lead around the head of 202, tucks it in the halter. He takes the sack and shovel from the child, lifts the child off. The cow steps into the stream. Drinks.

Play or not, the old man says. I'm going to take a moment.

The old man lays on the bank. The sack behind his head.

Downstream a large pool swells. Leaf litter slowing into it, spinning idly. A fisherman stands at the bottom, head bent over a fly he is tying to the tippet. Stares at the cow as his fingers work. He waves.

The old man waves back. We'll be moving soon enough, he shouts.

The fisherman pins the fly to his jacket. Digs out nail clippers to trim the excess line. He shouts, the fish may have never seen a Friesian before. Wouldn't know enough to be afraid of it. He squirts gel on his fingers. Rubs it into the fly. Besides, I believe this is a case where any inconvenience is warranted by the novelty of it.

The old man lifts his hand again. He turns and watches the child. The child stands in the river, off the bank. Stares back. The cow laps at the water and lifts it over her topline by jerking her head. He is still watching the child as he drifts to sleep.

The old man twitches and jolts as dark shapes drift across his mind. The heels of his boots dig into the sedge as he twists, leaving crescent cuts in the ground below him. He moans, a rising sound in his ribs that swells his chest. His arm rises and collapses against his side, as if, where he is, he is both the one swinging and being struck. His mouth open, slack-jawed. He starts to turn but folds onto his back again. The child, the child he utters, thrusting again.

The old man jerks awake. His eyes wide, dart around. His heart loud. He clutches at the ground and pulls himself up.

The fisherman is gone. The black pool languid, still. The cow has pushed into some briar and lays in the shade. She chews her cud, her tail caught in the thorns. The child stands yet in the river, staring at him.

The old man exhales. Settles back in the grass.

Suddenly the surface of the pool breaks. Seven heads rise out of the water. Eyes burst open, searching. Lifting. Seven teenagers, rings echoing off their bodies in the river. Their arms long and glinting. Their faces rough-hewn, condensed and mean. They turn about themselves as they climb to shore.

The old man, sleep-dazed. Pushes further against the

bank. Blinks. Looks to the hurl in the grass but does not reach for it.

The teenagers move as a heaving stack. Water sliding down their pale chests, their bent lurching frames. A few spit into the weeds. They are no one the old man has seen before. They slap and prod at the naked backs of each other. Call out in baying sounds. One turns to him, silver-haired, keeps his eyes on him as they lean forward and climb the bank, trudging over the sedge grass.

THE BOG SLIDE

The old man walks the front of the shed after switching the milkers between cows. Watching the cars collect at the bog slide. He leans on the doorway, stoop and lank, stares until the milkers have been on too long. The crumbled road like a fallen ribbon, lost in the grass. He stops once while feeding the heifers, hears the faint voices, and then resolves to finish chores without stopping again. When he is done he sets the milkers to wash and walks the road. He leaves the child in the heifer shed. The child watches him go.

The old man stares at his wellies as he follows the lane. The manure heaving on the rubber. When he looks up he tilts and walks tilted, as if it is him and not the valley that is off kilter. That it is to him to plumb himself to what is in front of him. The soil overturned, the roots of the heather bared up. The landscape snagged as it shifts around him, turning, sliding away. Or the ground, the valley, the brush is still turning for all he knows. He looks down to his wellies.

By the time he comes upon them there are a handful of vehicles pulled off the shoulder and men standing at the edge of the heaved gley, looking into the empty valley. Callaghan, Feeney, McHugh. The priest. These men as things cast apart from it. The soil, though having dried under the flat sky, is yet with black lustre, a darkness flowing towards them.

The elderly shoemaker sits atop the bonnet of his Golf,

licking his lips. Others lean on the car, gaze out. The priest to the side. His elbows in his hands. His head down.

They glance to the old man but do not turn around to acknowledge him.

The earth broke open and what souls it might have loosed, says the shoemaker. Is that right, Priest?

Ay, says the priest.

Whatever has been lifted from the ground hangs above us now. Priest?

Ay.

Callaghan guffaws, kicks away broken tarmac. It tumbles into the muck.

McHugh turns to Callaghan. Sure won't the county be down. Take care of it and so.

When your women are grey and your dog has died of age. We can sort out our own, Callaghan says.

The old man steps forward. He leans, speaks to the heels of their shoes. I can smooth it down with a tractor bucket. It won't be elegant, sure, but.

Callaghan glances over his shoulder at the old man and then turns back. He grabs his belt, adjusting himself. The sedge, the bog grass, a thin wrapper half-discarded and folded in on itself. The branches of brush half-swallowed and straining out. Those gathered do not look away, as if doing so would allow the upturned soil to creep closer.

The shoemaker lifts a wrinkled hand towards the broken road in front of them. I knew plenty of people that went that way for this or that, never coming back.

Feeney nods his head gravely. The rest stand motionless, rigid. Finally, McHugh turns to the shoemaker. You mean they moved away?

The shoemaker looks into the distance, no longer interested in talking.

There's things out that way. Medicines and banks and barracks, Feeney says.

Callaghan half-turns to the old man, looks him over again. Callaghan's cheeks are red, thick with flesh. The old man meets his glare the way a bush dampens a stone pitched against it.

It's a sign of the end, the priest says. He nods towards the bog.

Callaghan turns to McHugh. What were you doing out this way anyway? You were here nearly as early as Feeney.

I have business.

This awakens the shoemaker. He stomps on his bonnet. Jesus, we were all our lives friends, Pat, and I've never known you to have business.

I do my grocerying there.

You don't, Pat.

In the big Tesco there.

We have our own SuperValu, sure, says the shoemaker. For now, anyway.

A few wagtails scatter along the slide. Land on the coarse cattail stalks tipped sideways. The road the men are separated from carries along the small hill, disappears with the edge of the valley. Bends away.

McHugh scratches the back of his neck. Inhales sharply. It's the frozen pizzas they have, see.

The priest looks down by leaning the whole of himself forward, his frame held at an uneasy angle to the earth. His large palm moves underneath his soutane, pushing and mounding the pale flesh of his chest beneath it. His head tilts. We have to see this for what it is, he says. What it means. He looks to the old man.

Well, says Feeney. There mightn't be anything I want out there, but I don't like this idea of being cut off. We get one set of wheels across all that and it'll be easier for the next.

Jays, McHugh says. That's probably fifty yards through all that nonsense.

The shoemaker leans forward, narrows his eyes. That's

74

probably fifty yards, he says.

Callaghan blows his cheeks out, sends a rush of air between his teeth. He rubs his hands, paces the edge of the soil. The size of him growing. Tips himself one side, then the next. Alright, who's going? Who wants to buck the wild? Pat?

There's something bigger here, the priest says.

Feeney? Callaghan says.

The old man pushes his way between Feeney and McHugh. Stands on the lip of the road. Would you just let me top it over first? he says. It would take me ten minutes to head back and get the Ford.

A low clattering behind them, too rough and insistent to be the song of a bog bird. It grows, and then the Renault of Jimmy Haskins emerges from the walls of the lane, winding through the open. They turn and watch it in the distance, like an insect crawling through field grass. Its coughs and wheezes more apparent as it nears. The crescent of Jimmy's forehead over the dashboard. Comes to a slow jolting halt in front of the slide. Jimmy rolls down the window, the glass moaning.

Jimmy, Callaghan says.

Jimmy nods. Straightens to be taller in the seat.

How's himself keeping? The shoemaker shouts, nodding towards the back.

Oh, Jimmy says. Then says, steady as ever.

You have an aunt out there, don't you Jimmy? Callaghan says.

I do, sure.

Jimmy Haskins leans out the open window and folds his arms over the door. Looks the old man over. The old man steps forward, as if called. Puts his hands on his hips.

They say you're crazy, Jimmy says. He spits into the weeds on the shoulder. Wipes the residue off his chin. The thing is, people around here love saying things. They say you're dangerous because you hit people with your hurl. I say, you can't say someone is something until you ask them first.

Jimmy fingers a chewing gum out of a can on the dash.

Sticks it in the back of his mouth. Pins it in his teeth. Are you crazy?

The old man folds his arms over his chest. Looks to the bog slide, the puckered earth. Then back to Jimmy. I don't know, he says.

Well, Jimmy says. That's an answer anyway.

Come on Jimmy, Callaghan says, his voice rising. He taps the bonnet of the car with a hard palm. We're getting you across this shite.

The other men get behind the car, swing their elbows to loosen their arms. The shoemaker slowly climbs down. McHugh props his shoulder against the bumper, while Feeney braces himself and plants his feet.

The end, the priest whispers. He rubs his chest harder.

Jesus, Priest, Jimmy Haskins says, rolling up the window.

Jimmy pushes on the throttle, leaning back to reach his runners all the way. The car jolts ahead and bellows as it tries to climb the first rise of ground. The men groan and lean into it as they push it over and catch up to it and push again. Soil spits over their shoes. The car heaving. The old man finds an open spot on the boot and shoves into it.

Callaghan spins off the car and faces him. Would you fuck off? We know the boy did it. Would you fuck off? Callaghan turns to the priest. You lending yourself or what, Priest?

The priest takes his hand from his soutane. Runs his fingers over his face. Glances up at the old man, then away. They make room for the priest on the Renault.

The car spins ahead, bobbing over the terrain, sinking. The men fall in behind it and throw their weight at it again. The Colonel sits up in the backseat, looks around red-faced, and then lays down again. The car leaves deep tracks over the sloughed ground. Tipped at an angle. Inching towards the horizon.

COW TAKES SICK

The old man knees 202 in the ribs. She lifts her head off the straw, lays it down. He knees her again. Come on now, you whore. She stretches her neck, rises.

He slips the halter over her face. Around her drawn eyes, ridged pools drying in the daylight. Hands the end of the rope to the child, the child leads her out of the front of the shed. She follows him. Sharp pin bones, open ribs, slack-barrelled. A slouching beast.

From the sick pen she has stuck her head out the open window of the shed every day. Not watching the old man approach or the cats slink under the eaves but staring into the east. Dull eyes on the horizon. Her neck stretching from the shed as if the shed is her body, cracking around her.

Should have sent her in, the old man knows. And because he knows it he thinks he is soft. Old. He opened her sagging jaws, reached into her with a magnet and plunged it into the darkness of her reticulum. Poured calcium in. Everything falling silently to exhaustion inside her. He'll put her in a paddock by the road with good grass, good grass an act of kindness as the old man understands it. Their footsteps echo in the driveway. The cow reaches over to sniff the skull, then keeps walking.

A dark green lorry drives down the lane. Sidling on worn tyres. The fat arm of Geir Sullivan out the window, emerging from his silhouette. His eyes inside the cab like tarnished rivets, considering the child, considering the cow. He drives by twice a day, turns right at the end of the lane. Traces the boundaries of the old man's property. As if he can cut it away.

The old man stands at the end of his driveway. Watching

exorcism

Geir Sullivan. Geir Sullivan watching him.

The exhaust from the Ford coils and rises. Twists until it joins the grain dust sky at some hazy layer above the bog. The old man lowers himself over a stack of turf, clutches the bottom pieces, and lifts the pile towards the crawling tractor. Lowers and lifts again, his arms bowed in stiff angles. The ground wheezes with moisture underneath his wellies. Is drawn back to the earth as his footsteps fade behind him. The old man reaches into the cab, turns the Ford in a slow arc to begin another pass. Has just righted the tractor when the Honda Civic pulls along the shoulder.

The priest holds his garments tight across the tops of his wellies as he steps over the matgrass in the ditch. The purple stole lifts off him, settles again. He clutches the crucifix dangling over his chest, weaves through the rows of bundled turf. Lumbering, bulging figure curtained in black, the cloth drifting across the sedge. The old man reaches into the cab and pulls the stopper by the child's legs. The machine stills. The apparition of the motor-hum floating in the silence. The priest and farmer face each other on the bog.

You were right, Mulgannon, the priest says.

The old man presses the hurl into the ground, steadies himself.

I've been turned gutless, the priest says. You put a light to that. He looks into the back of the trailer. Does not let the air deflate from this chest as he breathes.

I'm not asking for an apology and I'm not going to give one, the old man says.

The child climbs out of the tractor. Holds the grab bar in one hand, his hurl in the other. The wood dragging over the steps. The child's nimble movements dampened by the slack clothes fitted over him. Jumps off the last step, the skull rocking on his head.

The priest does not look at the child but fixes on a point above him. The slope of his forehead glinting with damp. When the priest holds up the crucifix in front of him it is above the hill line and alone in an empty sky.

Man, God and Devil, he says. The five of us will settle it now.

You're mad, the old man says.

What would you have me do? the priest says. He still holds the crucifix in the air. Looks around him as if he expects the hedges to stir. The turf stacks to collapse around them.

The old man's face tightens. The tractor stands behind them on the bog plane. The door still open. He places his hurl in front of the child.

I call upon Jesus Christ, with the power of the Almighty.

Do not, the old man says.

A rook rises out of a distant hedgerow, cuts a soundless path across the sky. The two men watch it disappear into a stand of alders.

The priest sits down on the step of the tractor. He reaches into his undercloth, fumbles. Pulls out a cigarette like a small bone plucked from his body. Leans on his knees as he lights it. Breathes in.

The old man doesn't loosen his grip on the hurl as he watches the priest. The priest staring at the bog weed. Smoke curling from his nostril and spreading over his face. His lips move, a faint echo of thought. A man deciding something. He tucks his undercloth neatly into his wellies. Then crushes the cigarette under the rubber heel and stands.

I command you, unclean spirit, whoever you are –

Get a hold of yourself, the old man says.

Speak, demon, the priest barks. Speak! To what purpose do you insolently resist? To what purpose do you brazenly refuse? You are guilty before the Almighty, whose laws you have transgressed. You are guilty before the whole human race.

The old man lifts the hurl from the ground and swings it.

It hits the priest in the head. The priest jerks. Shields his face with one hand, lifts the crucifix with the other. Why do you stand and resist, knowing as you must that the Almighty brings your plans to nothing?

The old man swings again. It strikes the priest in the side. The priest tries to grab the hurl but the old man yanks it free. The old man stands in front of the child.

The priest crosses himself. In the name of the Father, the Son, and the Holy – it has to be done! the priest shouts as the old man feigns with the hurl.

The priest steps towards the child and the old man puts the shaft to his chest and pushes him back. Nearly falls himself from the momentum. The priest raises the crucifix again, reaches out. The old man leans back and swings the flat of the hurl. It strikes the hand that holds the cross and sends it tumbling through the air until it sinks into a hedgerow.

What would you have me do? the priest yells. He grabs two pieces of turf, holds them perpendicular, and lunges at the child. The old man has only enough time to step into his path before they both fall to the ground at the child's feet.

The priest reaches the turf towards the child. Give place, he says, thrashing over the body of the old man. Saliva spurting from the edge of his lips. Give way! The old man pulls at the priest's elbows and presses his chin into the side of his ribs. The skin on the priest's arm bleached white from being pulled taut. The cords rising in the old man's neck. His tongue straining from a gaping mouth.

The ground beneath them stirs, shifts. The land splays open as wet soil flows across the valley.

The child standing at the foot of the bog slide. His hurl in the grass.

THE OLD MAN SINGS

The old man runs a pen knife through the white plastic on the bale. Moves through it smoothly. Unzipping it.

After he balls the plastic in his arms and casts it aside he takes a pitchfork and thrusts it into the bale. He lets it stick in there, half-expects blood to come out. And then draws it free and starts undressing it, dragging hay to the yearlings.

The cattle crowd along the bunk and strain for it. The old man sings while he pulls it to them. Heifer, heifer, you're a dumb slut, always wanting hay up front. He fills half of the bunk with forage and then stops. Looks up to the sky through the dusty windows. Stabs the fork into the bale again.

He kicks at the stones among the gravel and they scatter out of his way, bounding, until they sink into the lawn grass. Swipes his hurl in front of him with both hands as he steps, grunting aloud. Swings left, swings right. Picks up an old can of WD40 lying in the weeds, tosses it in the air, and bats it into the hedge. He stops at the end of his driveway and stands with his hand on his hips.

After a few minutes Geir Sullivan's lorry creeps down the lane, heaving. He leans his head out the window to stare at the old man as he passes, chewing. The flesh in his face rippling. Taps his fingers on the driver's side door. Lifts them at the old man, reaching towards him.

The old man puts the hurl on his shoulder. Turns to follow

the vehicle as it passes.

The old man watches the lorry until it is out of view. Then returns to the heifer shed, pulls the fork out. He gathers a mound of hay and takes it to the heifers. They shove against each other and push over the brisket bar. The old man rubs their foreheads. Sings, Oh Geir is not too bright, wait till I bollox him right.

THE
INSTRUMENTS
MISSING

The old man, the child, walk into the Clarke Martin. Tables half-dissolved in the pale light. The ends of the room fade away into silhouette, oblivion bleeding into the edge of view. Dust hangs in the grey air by the windows, waiting to be pulled by someone's breath. On the bar, lamplight skidding off wood panels. Vacant chairs spread across the floor, all facing some empty wall.

In one corner sit the politician and O'Donnell. The politician forward on his elbows, O'Donnell arched back over the chair, watching the old man, the child, pass. On the other side, Gill, Lonegan, Farrar. Slumped and prostrate until one lifts his head to talk. The conversations from both tables cross each other over the creaking floor. The child pulls a stool away from the bar, sits with the ex-farmers. As one apart. The old man picks up his pint, joins them as well.

The three aging men slouch, staring in angles. Gill lifts his finger to the old man. Well, you look wretched.

Worse than before, really, Lonegan says.

The old man looks at the child. Pulls on the belt loop to raise the child's trousers. The child pulls back. Same old song, he says. Have you nothing better?

Barely a conversation that isn't about you Íosac, Lonegan says.

Farrar says, talk and talk. About Íosac Mulgannon. He

grunts, nods his head at the other table. Refolds his arms.

The politician licks the Guinness head off his lip. He taps a beer mat at O'Donnell. A duck's quack doesn't echo and no one knows why, he says.

Would you fuck off.

Do you think he's really cursed, then? the politician says. Touched, so?

The boy?

Some odd sky around here.

O'Donnell shakes his head. Pauses. Then shakes it again. He's just a boy. And that's weather. Science, like. He stares at the back of the child sitting on the stool. Did he really just show up one night?

That's the story.

Whose? Mulgannon's?

Malachy pushes through the rear door. It cleaves and snaps behind him. They're gone. He throws up his hands, his shirt pulled tight against his paunch. They're god damn gone. Then he's through the door again. Cursing.

I'm afraid of death, Lonegan says. He looks at the other men. I am, but I don't see myself dying. But Íosac, you do.

You're saying I'm a bit mental.

If you weren't you'd keep better company, Gill says.

The old man reaches through the bone, touches the child on the face. The child recoils. Ran over by the rota-spreader once, he says. Sleeve got caught on the auger before. I've been knocked in the head more than a few times. Bit of a cruel joke still being around, all in all.

Farrar starts laughing. A derisive cackle, rising. He lifts off the seat. Finally settles, belly-still.

If there's something bigger than all this it should have taken me by now, the old man says.

Malachy comes back. Red-faced, dim-eyed. He puts a towel over his head and leans against the whiskey stand. Those instruments sat along the back bench there for as long as I had this place. The cloth over his mouth folds and refolds as he talks. Now they're gone. Taken, it seems.

The child lowers himself off the stool. He walks slowly between the tables, one step at a time, dragging his feet. He tips his head back, swings it side to side. The shadow-pits of the open eyes scanning the room, his own breath grazing over the flat teeth. The skull always in a pained, bawling phrase.

The politician wrinkles his brow. Glances at Malachy and then back to his companion.

Some state of things, O'Donnell mutters.

All natural and so, the politician says. Sure, now. Sure.

O'Donnell moves his shoulders against the back of the chair. It creaks loudly, resounding between the panel walls, until he sets himself again. Mulgannon, he's a bit off, sure. But the boy. An unsanctioned love affair, you think?

Could he have been hers, sent over from London? Hers and his, I mean?

Mulgannon's never said anything. Not that I know of.

Malachy puts down fresh pints on the table of the politician and O'Donnell. Then on the table of the white-haired men. Drink, won't you? Sad day, Lads. Someone might as well have some good from it.

The child passes Malachy. The skull swings its fleshless gaze over him. Silent. Turns away.

Gill grabs the arm of the old man and clutches it tight. You're already gone, Íosac Mulgannon. I'm not going to say goodbye to you yet. But I'm not going to be surprised when the news comes.

Lonegan tenders the new pint to the side. I'll speak for myself or for the table, as seen fit, but I want to say that we were always friends of yours.

The shapes of the people outside pass through the lettering on the fogged window. Drift by soundless. Inside, old bale hooks, sickle blades, rake wheels suspended over the patrons, give texture to the shadows above. A clock hangs on the wall, its glass dusty. The numbers vague behind it. In a corner a fireplace that is not lit.

I was thinking the other day, O'Donnell says. Mulgannon is in a tight spot, now isn't he? You could see why he wouldn't send the boy away, mad or no.

Do you think he's taking care of the boy in the right way?

The welfare lady seemed to think otherwise.

The child passes by the politician, causing him to hunch down and whisper towards O'Donnell. Did she ask it like that?

You have to be a bit human about it all, O'Donnell says.

You do! You do! says the politician.

But then there's the bigger picture. The greater good and all.

The boy or the all of us, if that's the way it is. Is that what you're saying? The politician rips his beermat into four pieces and then stacks them. Part of me feels for Mulgannon, the politician says. Mad or no. I get it, see.

The duck's quack. Is that shite now?

The politician shrugs. Read it on a cereal box.

The front door swings open. A handful of townspeople push into the Clarke Martin, cluttering around the bar. Are they gone? Jesus, Malachy. Are they gone? A few take off their hats, knead them in their hands. They look about them as if seeing the pub for the first time. The Sheehan leans against the wall with one arm, his head down.

Gallagher runs her hand along the fabric of the empty bench. By God, they're gone.

Like the fecking wind, Malachy says. He opens the dishwasher just to slam it shut.

The patrons settle between the two occupied tables. They drape their coats over their legs, nod at the elderly men on one side, the politician and O'Donnell on the other. Fold their hands on the table as they wait to be served. Their stares inevitably pulled to the bare wall that once held up banjos and fiddles.

The Sheehan is the last person standing. They were here ever since I remember and now they're not. He shakes his head and finally sits down.

The old man grabs the child, pulls him onto his knee. Clench-fisted on the child's waistline to still him. Twists the fabric in his hand. The skull faces him. Feigns at him as if to bite.

The thin rushing noise of the Guinness tap and an occasional sigh. A stray creak in the floorboards. The townspeople stoop over their own arms laying flaccid on the table. They awaken only to take the pint Malachy hands to them. Faces down, sagging, like rocks overturned by the plough. Carty pulls on his beard. They'll have the Barrys from our press before long.

Gill stands, scans the room. He catches the eye of the politician. Says to him, did you know that the Icelanders came and took the best looking women off us long ago? They proved it.

The politician straightens. Looks to O'Donnell and then to Gill. They'd hardly be back for more.

That's the thing, Gill says, lifting a finger. Drawing the politician closer. They know we wouldn't expect it now.

A few murmurs spread across the room. Some clutch their pints, pull them a little tighter.

Jaysus, they got away with it once, Gill says. That's all I'm saying.

The Sheehan rises slowly, the table shaking from his grip, and stands over the empty bench. He bends and clutches at something unseen, but when he turns around and moves his fingers everyone understands he is plucking the banjo that isn't there. The shape of their loss in his hands. He closes his eyes in concentration. No one knew that he could play.

Magee stands beside him and unlatches a violin. The silence is greater now, coming from two instruments. Magee's arm sways in an even line and some of those seated are tipped to and fro with it. The King girl is a guitar player, one of the town's best, and so some glance in her direction until she sighs and rises too.

The unplayed melody washes over the bar. It fills those listening and swells inside them. The musicians keep it steady and in time. The words that aren't sung tell about the things they already know, and of things they don't want to put names on. It drifts between them, pulling on them. No one taps their foot. No whooping. Those seated glance at the others around them and smile mournfully and turn back to the performance.

No one stirs as the musicians put their instruments away and sit down.

READING

The child and the old man lay side by side. In the dark. The old man's hands holding the book in front of him, disembodied by shadow. Reads. The first warp-spasm seized Cúchulainn, and made him into a monstrous thing, hideous and shapeless, unheard of. His body made a furious twist inside his skin, so that his feet and shins and knees switched to the rear and his heels and calves switched to the front. The child still, motionless. The old man looks over to see that the eyes of the child are still open and they are. The old man turns the page. When that spasm had run through the high hero Cúchulainn he stepped into his sickle war-chariot that bristled with points of iron and narrow blades.

The old man bunches the duvet and props the book on it. Grabs the hurl. Slaps its face into his palm and then slaps it again. In that style, then, he drove out to find his enemies and did his thunder-feat and killed a hundred, then two hundred, then three hundred, then four hundred, then five hundred.

The whole bed jolts. Louder. The child is shook as he lays. Rocking in the sheets.

THE TAIL PAINT

The old man walks along the bunks, clearing the cows from the alley to scrape the shed. The smell of musty fermentation pushed from their mouths in even draws. He leans on the brisket bar, reaches the hurl forward, taps on a cow's loin. Limps ahead. Leans on the bar, reaches the hurl again. The cows step back, untangle themselves from the group, gingerly feel for space with their back legs. Pass through the open gate, to the pasture.

One Friesian lifts up on her rear feet, mounts another cow. Hooves scrape against the concrete. The old man sits on the windowsill, slumping. Its cobwebs clinging to his back. The cow on top thrusts her pelvis, her teats swinging below her. Then dismounts. Settles herself before lifting her chin off the back of the other cow.

The old man leans on the glass, the hurl against his knee. He watches the mounted cow, finds himself looking through her. Finally says, wait now. He grabs the tail paint and follows after her.

She stands, her loin flexing as if bracing again. The old man puts a red X on her hind leg, to remember to breed her tomorrow. The mark like a wound, torn flesh. He slaps her thigh but she doesn't move.

The vacuum of the wash tank shuts off. Followed by the shed lights. The heifers begin to lie in their pens, putting their knees down and then tucking their rear legs, having been grained. The dusk-to-dawn light on the front of the cubicle shed starts to flicker and then settles into a dull purple glow in the dusk.

The old man leaves the shed, trudges the worn path to the house. Head down. His hurl drags behind him in the grass. A handful of cows still linger near the gate. Between them, across their bodies, the words Emma, Ache, I, Sometimes.

THE OLD
MAN DISKS

The old man disks. Pulls the coulters over the ground he has ploughed, pulls apart the magnetism of the earth, its affinity for itself, makes the ground suitable for planting. Ryegrass for summer hay. He turns off the lane, lowers the disk. Disks.

He drives the Ford. Keeps the frontend loader on because he likes to have his work before him, not look behind at a hitch. The tractor has aged, weathered. Is small and light, but has its call on soft ground. More than that, the old man takes it out to see that it still goes. That it is not fragile and only for the shed.

The first pass of the tractor along the lane, the outer edge of his field darkened with upturned soil, the colour drifting off. The ground lifting and falling wetly. The sagging fence along the lane, shaped around Nancy O'Rourke's pasture, is gone. As is the scrub brush. The paddock has been ploughed, disked. A bride dragged to a sudden marriage. Young John Allen traces the contour of the field with his planter, planting corn.

When the breeze blows the old man receives it through the open windows, abridged. Other times it is the exhaust that surrounds him. Fills him. A figure inside the rattling glass. A shape bent forward.

Young John's planter plants six rows at a time. Young John, the old man thinks. A new-born calf stumbling towards the teat. The old man looks over his shoulder, checks the disk.

Steadies the front wheel. The old man supposes Young John should not be blamed.

The ground is soft. The tractor wheels tunnel small channels in the earth that are raked over by the coulters. The stir of the engine is loud. So is the prattle of metallic joints behind him. It is a ceaseless rumble that slides between the inside of the skull and the images pressed against it. A lubrication that sends his thoughts spinning. His body settles into the rhythms of work. Swaddled by the vibration of the machine.

The pleasure of fieldwork is that he cannot wonder, cannot feel like he should be doing something else, more, because there is nothing more he can do than go to the end of the field, turn around, and go to the other end. And the old man goes to the end of the field with the disk. The bucket bobs in front of the tractor as the tractor rocks from the strain. Over the roughness of the hurled land. He stares ahead, over the right front wheel, uses it as his sextant to keep himself, the tractor, straight, but really finds himself gazing off at some vague point above the bonnet and below the horizon. Allen, that cunt.

The old man looks over his shoulder. At the soil that is cultivated, the soil that is not, and the coarse border between them. He will have to dress the field a second time, maybe a third, because his disk is light. His shoulders begin to ache in the familiar way, the primal chant ricocheting inside his skin. The old man disks, and will disk until the field is done. Ready to be seeded.

Allen is smug, the old man decides, as their two tractors jostle in parallel, only the lane between them. The old man looks at him. Allen stares ahead, at the field he works. He is not a man tested and tried, and therefore not worthy. He does not struggle as good men do, does not feel the hunger, pain inside. He is not a man called, but to which it is given. The lane that separates them is a line that pre-existed them. One already in place as they came upon it. Allen's tractor is faster, heavier. It passes the Ford, reaches the headlands, and turns away.

The old man moves along the ground. The fog of exhaust surrounds him, clothes him, puts the things around him in a haze. A settled heat upon him. Rooks circle behind him, loud. Prod at the turned soil. The old man is juddered in the seat. Atop the currents of the world that stretch over it. Inside him runs a fence line pulled off its insulators. The old man has stood. He is the rock they turn the ploughs around. The old man is a bundle of rhythms that echo over the valley. The old man is.

The hands of the old man grip the wheel, turn it suddenly over the lane. The coulters rattle and scrape against the road. Are just as quickly muted as the old man guides it along the edge of Young John's field. The old man stands on the top step. The tractor presses ahead, on its own.

The tractor of Young John eases to a halt, his planter stilling. He opens his door. Peers out with a hand on the grab bar.

The old man pulls his belt strap. His trousers wither at his ankles. He lifts a stream of piss into the paste-grey horizon. Falling to Allen's ground.

Young John a silhouette inside his machine. His knees, his wellies, the rest falling to shadow. A figurine with its face glazed a single colour. A dismembered weed blows against his front tyre, is pulled away. His door closes.

The old man turns into his own field. Doubles back to continue the pass made with the disk. Falls into place and disks. His hands gripping the steering wheel, kneading it, his vision on the front tyre and it turns, turns. He snorts and snaps mucous on the floor, the edge of the seat. Keeping the Ford straight. The disk bounces over stones, leaves marks over the top of them. He looks over his shoulder and there is the John Deere, the tractor of Young John Allen, charging across the soil.

The John Deere is in road gear. The seed boxes behind it bounce up and down like fingers drummed on a knee. Shifts and goes faster. Jerks as it crests the risen boundary of the lane.

Young John Allen thrusts into the old man's field, his tractor heaving. He lowers the planter without slowing, the marking arm swung down to cleave the ground around it.

The old man pushes the clutch. Watches through a dusty window.

Young John drops seed around the old man. He swings in a wide, violent arc, the coulters in the front of the machine pulling apart the ground and the back of it pressing in the kernel. A contamination that will spring corn plants in his hayfield. Six lines traced in the disked and undisked ground. Fallen rainbow of the colourless sky. Young John Allen shouts behind the heavy glass, but it is drowned out by his own engine. The planter lifts just before crashing over the lane again.

The old man, the old man, he is one called. To stand, against the times, to remain, resist and be counted as one that had to be slain because he would not kneel, submit. To be found not wanting. He descends the steps of the Ford, a man emerging from the dark haze to champion, fight. He circles behind his machine, pulls the pin of the disk, and drops it in the clay.

The Ford howls as the old man pushes the throttle to its reach, the seat below him shaking, feigning, pulling at the reigns. He lifts his wellies and the Ford lurches. Bouncing over the field. Bucket raised, poised. The hydraulic lines along the arms like tendons stretched taut. Smalls wheels spinning, spinning. Throwing the ground of Young John's field behind him. Marring the planted rows, cutting into them, fouling their edges.

The John Deere paces forward, steeping the soil. Young John stands on the top step, grabs the lip of the bonnet. He looks over it at the old man coming.

The Ford turns in.

Young John sees it. Freezes. Stares. He jerks his machine to a halt. The old man turns sharper.

The narrow bucket pierces the planter, springing a yellow shatter of plastic and seed. Shards pitch into the air like turning blades. The coils give, fling. One leaps into the sky like a brown trout, over the John Deere's cab, and falls to the soil. The planter rocks, tilts. The wheels of the Ford spin and push and push. The bucket drives into the frame of the equipment. Finally snaps the tongue, toppling it.

Young John Allen pounds on the bonnet. His eyes heated stone. He screams but the whine of the John Deere's engine floods his words. The old man reverses.

The old man stands on the steps of his tractor as he drives away. A figure cast openly against the grey horizon.

THE OLD MAN AND CHILD WALK IN THE DARK

The old man at the kitchen table in the dark. Pulls on his wellies, heels sliding in the rubber, finding their shape. Clumps of mud fall to the lino and shatter. He pushes the hurl off the floor and rises. The lino below the edge of the table heavy with pocked dents. Empty eye sockets, looking up to the old man. The child stands in the hallway. The old man slips on his cap, steps onto the lawn. The door open behind him.

Come on then, he says, crossing the driveway.

Their wellies clap off the lane in the night. The child steps a little behind, like an echo trailing the old man. The old man fed twine through the belt loops and knotted it to keep the child's trousers tight. Rolled up the sleeves of his geansaí and sometimes stops to fold them again, against the child's pull. When he lets go the child walks with his head down. The skull swaying side to side and searching the darkness.

Clouds seal over the sky and dampen the moon. Everything in degrees of shadow and the idea of things and not the things themselves. Blackberries couched in the brush, half-concealed in the branches. The old man picks them as he passes. Hand plunging the leaves without fear of thorns, bristles, plucking them with short, deft motions. He holds them out for the child, but the child does not look at his hand.

Trees tilting in the hedgerows. Hay fields rustle. The ghosts of the landscape made uneasy, stirring and closing in. The smell of old stone rises from the walls around them. The old man throws a berry at the child. It bounces off the ivory curve of the bone's temple. The child winces. Bats at the darkness. The old man throws another one, but the child does not react.

Originally Keane thought it was coincidence that every time he got up to piss at night it was when Íosac Mulgannon went by. Maybe it was at first. Now they are either synchronized in some odd, queer way, or Mulgannon has a gravity that pulls on the people around him.

Keane is not sure that he can actually make out the features in the dark, and that they are sad and lonely, or just thinks he sees them and figures that's how they are. There's plenty of lost old lads in the world, Keane thinks. But Mulgannon, well. He's more turned about than most. Hell, sure what does anyone know?

He used to be normal once. Keane heard that much, so. That would have been before the boy, anyway. When someone from another part of the country orphaned the lad. Jaysus, dropped him off at the shed like a cat no one wanted. Keane thinks he heard that, anyway. And Jaysus, Keane thinks. Now Mulgannon's outside my window when I piss. Out there in the dark, looking for things as he knew them.

The child's wellies leave stains on the road, the wet of blackberries. Dark half-circles that follow after him like the tracks of an animal. He keeps his head down. Swings his small limbs sombrely. The old man clicks his hurl against the walls. Glances at the child. Then, in a burst, the old man throws his shoulder into him. The child falls to the ground.

The skull looks up to him, open-mouthed.

Toughen up, now.

The old man wedges the hurl under the thighs of the child, scoops him up with the flat of the head. Forces the child to his feet. The old man freezes, arms suspended. Thinks he heard something behind them. The child reluctantly catches himself, keeps walking.

Devaney sits at the kitchen table. Steam rising from the cup of tea in front of him, twisting around his knuckles. He's out there again, he yells towards the bedroom.

Why do you wait for him? Her voice comes through the closed door, muffled. Go to bed.

Devaney opens a packet of Bourbon Creams. Bites one in two. Chews in silence. Every time he looks away he has to stare through his own reflection to see Mulgannon and the boy again. The farmer drags the hurl behind him and if Devaney listens carefully he can hear it scraping. A lonely keening into the night. The child walks close to him, at his side. Always at his side.

He is a man at the end, Devaney thinks. And that would throw anyone off. The first night he had seen the old man walk by he had the impression he was a man measuring who he was and what he had become. In the years since Devaney has not changed his mind. He has seen it in other men. People, getting older, for whom life seems more uncertain instead of more settled. The past floods into the present until it's a struggle to keep them in different corners. It would throw anyone off. A walk helps to clear the head.

Is he gone yet? a voice shouts from the bedroom. Would you go to bed?

Whitethorns lean over the top of the stone walls. Into the alley. Because of it the alley seems much higher above them, themselves much deeper in it. The old man enjoys the stillness of the night, of being the only thing that moves through it. But it also makes him uneasy. You're a sour thing, he tells the child. Jerks at the child, but the child does not flinch. Steps at the child again. His chest out. His fists half-raised. The child smiles. Stares up to him with the skull half-tipped.

You think I'm weak? the old man shouts.

He runs at the child with the hurl and the child runs in front of him.

Mary Flaherty shudders, a cold chill running along her

side, and that's how she knows Íosac is passing by. She crosses herself. She stands along the wall, looking through slits in the curtain. She is careful not to make contact with the folds in the fabric and signal her presence. She is not one to draw attention to herself. The windowsill is crowded with half-burned candles, but there is a space for her hand as she leans forward.

Íosac's mother had told her mother once that she had meant for him to be a good man, and so she wanted to name him Isaac. It was a time in the country when you couldn't give your children English names though. Mary still believes he's a good man, deep down. But he is one possessed. It is the child, she knows. The child has turned him around and off-kilter, because of the things he would do for the child. A dark attachment Íosac confuses for love. He is not the children Íosac would have had, had he left the island. If he made different choices. She lights a candle again as he passes by her window. Then watches as a black dog slinks behind them, its head bent low.

THE CAR PARK

202 stops over a puddle, a flooded corner of the car park in town. Dissolves her own reflection by drinking from it, inhaling rainwater in long draws. The white lines below the pool emerging again. The old man takes the child off her back and sets him in the water. Splashes it towards the child, onto his trousers, playing. The skull looks up to him.

The old man's father would take him to town when he was the age of the child. The town a strange, unfamiliar place where people leaned in doorways silently and did not plant things. He watched his father and brother leave for it on bicycles every week or two, and wondered about it while they were gone. When he was old enough to go he stared at the rowed houses, concrete structures. At the sweet shop, the market, and the people who passed without saying hello. At that age he marvelled at the town and swore that he would never live there.

202 flicks her tongue absently at the pool and the old man decides she is done and pulls her across the car park. Taking the halter on one side, the child's hand in the other. Stale water clings to the hair on the cow's chin, drops to the tarmac as her head swings. The lot empty and cracking, stretched between declining buildings. The child taking exaggerated steps to match the pace of the old man, the cow.

An old grey Peugeot bounds through the opposite entrance of the car park. Faded paint, dented bonnet. Rushing towards them. The old man continues ahead and then hesitates when the car does not turn. The vehicle hits a pothole, jerks front to back, does not slow. A hand out the window points at them.

The old man jerks the child right but collides into the cow's front leg. The glare of the windscreen conceals those behind it, flickers as it rocks. The engine raising in pitch as it thrusts ahead. The old man turns the other way but has not thought to drop the lead rope and 202 cannot follow his pull quickly enough. The Peugeot upon them.

The old man turns his back, flinches.

The battered car veers and then turns sharply, circling at full speed. The tyres shriek, leave dark scars. Haze rises from the tread. The old man looks up to see the Peugeot crammed with teenagers, glaring at him. The steering wheel cranked as they spin furiously. The old man holds the child, the cow, and turns with the vehicle. 202 kicks her legs out and jolts wide-eyed, her hooves landing on the tarmac like gunfire. The old man tangles in the rope, trips. Exhaust explodes from the whirling car, joins the smoke from the howling tyres, is black and heavy. One boy, lanky ginger, now lays over the legs of the others in the back and they heave his torso out the window. His arms reaching towards the child in the haze, a crazed sneer on his face. He bites at the air.

The old man dizzies, stumbles. Grabs the cow's neck as he collapses.

The car speeds off, shattering the puddle on its way out of the car park. The hand still pointing. Crude laughter trailing it.

THe
ISPCA

The loader bounces down the lane. Bucket in the air, the chain's end dangles in front of him like the fraying threads of the tractor. The vibrations of the machine pass through the old man's loins. Makes him taller, wider. The dust of the cab carried between the walls with him, suspended inside the glass. The old man stares ahead, unblinking.

He pushes on the clutch. The tractor's momentum swings it into the paddock, through the open gate and along the fence line. He stops.

Someone stands over 202.

A round-shouldered woman, large. She stoops forward like something suddenly reared up on its hind legs. She leans to the cow and takes pictures of it. Electric shocks of light over the slumped creature, 202 with its mouth, tongue out. The only sound the quiet gas weaving inside it. The woman has curly hair fringed over a broad face.

The old man jumps out of the tractor. Hurl dragging behind him. He lifts it up.

He starts to swing.

Íosac Mulgannon? ISPCA.

The woman carries a notebook, writes in it. She doesn't offer her hand.

The old man rocks on his feet. Lifts the hurl higher.

Is this your animal, Mr. Mulgannon?

He looks her over. Runs his tongue back and forth along his teeth. Finds it pulsing there.

Is this your animal, Mr. Mulgannon?

He exhales. Leans on the hurl instead. Fits back into the shape of himself. Was, he says. I believe it's God's now.

He bends in closer to her. Squints. To face him what darkness must be inside her? He looks her over again.

Heavy air, pale day. The grey sky turns the world into an empty shed. The dead pile behind him, the trees that bend over it and glinting bones emerging from the hedge grass. But they are here, on this empty plane. Man, woman, cow.

The woman says, would you like to comment on the condition of the animal?

Hardly died of a broken heart, the old man says.

You're stating that the animal was well looked after? She writes more.

A heat passes over him. His breath snags. You can't ask me that.

She glances up to him, pauses.

You a farmer then? he says.

ISPCA. She taps her badge with a brusque flick.

You're not a farmer then you'd hardly know cows and what befalls them. Was it Allen then? He called it in?

To stand there as she does, to oppose him and give him something to oppose. To scowl and push against him. He is old, but, as she now shows him, not void of natural welling.

The woman says nothing. She flips a page and takes notes. The old man leans towards her notebook. She bends away. He shifts on his feet and jabs his hurl into the ground.

Her breath blows over her upper lip, is audible. The tart smell of chlorine rises around her where she sterilized her boots going into farms and out of them. She tips her head from one side to the next, something under her skin grinding against itself. She sighs. The old man would spit onto the ground if his mouth was not so dry.

What'd she have? the woman asks.

Not hardware, no milk fever. Sometimes you just don't know. Didn't catch from the bull, for all her trying.

So you didn't contact a vet then?

Four hundred quid to have her die the same?

Are you saying you did not have the funds available to properly care for this animal? She looks up to him suddenly. The muscles in her neck reverberate. Her clothes flex and release as she breathes.

He says, I'm saying I know what a vet is good for and what he is not.

You don't scare me.

Her shape is a thick layer of heft and nothing inside but darkness. When he enters her he will be in there alone. The world is a grey flat common they stand on but inside her, he thinks. A pool of hot shadows. And when he leaves her the darkness will pour out of her and swallow them all and he would be ready for it.

Get off my place, the old man says. You haven't the right to be here.

She again lifts the laminated name card clipped to her shirt. She doesn't look up from scrawling on the paper.

The old man quivers. His head tilted back. His waist tips forward, imperceptibly.

He says, can you be so daft as to not see this as a setup job? Do you know Young John?

Mr. Mulgannon.

You're not listening to me.

She continues to write. He puts the flat of his hurl on her notebook. She lets the papers fall to her side, grasping them with a large hand. Glares at him like a parent admonishing a child.

He grimaces, then rolls his head around, slowly. The flash of his bright eyes looking at her. She is a heavy thing. She stands before him, calling herself his opposite. Staring at the cut of her pulls him into pacing, gripping his hurl tightly in both hands. Crushing the pasture grass beneath him. The call heavy on the old man. The things that move the world lying in wait, prone. Asking, and asking of him. An axle snaps inside him, slips a joint. For him to be someone who stands, and she a thing bending before him. For him to be. He throws his hands up. Hurries back to the tractor.

When he returns she's on one knee, taking pictures. Close-ups of the bloating head, nude teeth. Her pant leg wet with pasture moisture. The rubber of her wellies bent, sleek and raw. He has a hacksaw.

She stands up quickly. Mr. Mulgannon, you'll have an opportunity to state your case.

You're not listening to me.

He stands, head-cocked, the blade tilted and pressing into his trousers. He breathes, audible. A sigh expanding between them.

He bends, places the saw at the base of the cow's ear. He runs the ribbed steel into the flesh, tearing into it. The tag that reads 202 jolts up and down. Convulses. The cartilage opens, pink, foul, flaccid. The ear leans away from the skull. The old man grabs it and severs the last of the ropey tissue.

The old man stands up, pulls out the plastic number tag. It falls to the paddock grass. He wrenches baling twine through the punched hole. Ties the ends together like a pendant.

You're not listening to me, he says. This will help.

He slips the ear over her.

The woman stumbles backwards. He holds the twine between his fingers, but it is thrust out of his grasp. The ear swings against her chest.

She rolls up her papers, sticks them in her back pocket. Spreads her legs and folds her arms. The ear settles, stills. She does not turn away, fidget. The full of her before him, unflinching. He swallows. She holds his glare as the breeze shifts her curls. The bottom of her teeth showing as she breathes discreetly through her mouth. Her arms wide, pulling at the fabric.

She slowly lifts the twine, ear off her chest. Tosses it to the grass at the old man's feet. Turns back to the vehicle.

The old man watches, gripping the hurl.

The old man is drawn towards the end of the field, the gate where her car, her curses have just left. The idea of them still swelling. He takes slow strides, wipes his hands on his jeans. Grabs at a fence post, leans on it.

Pressing his forehead into the back of his hand he exhales. Drops his hurl.

THE
FESTIVAL

They stand around a square of rope, the rope held up by old milk cans in the corners. The grass inside spray-painted into smaller squares with numbers. A paper is passed, a hat, each man tucking his pint under his elbow to scratch his name and drop a fiver. Passes it on.

The old man and the child stand back. Watch from near the food trucks. The child holds a sweet bun in front of him that the old man has bought him. Does not look at it or eat it. The old man has put a poncho over the child in case it rains, but it has not rained. He stretched the collar to fit over the skull and then reshaped it with electrical tape. The plastic almost reaching the grass.

Young John Allen brings a heifer out of the back of a trailer, the animal pulling against the lead and then leaping out in a burst. The rope is lifted enough for Young John to drag her beneath it. He slips off her halter and leaves her on the marked grass. Glances at the old man and then half-turns so as not to see him.

The heifer stretches, sniffs at the rope. The men watch her silently, one hand in their pockets. The other pinning their glasses to their chest.

Two men walk on either side of Tom Healy as he stumbles out of the Clarke Martin to sing at the town's yearly festival. A few balloons on lampposts. A faded banner rolled out again and hung over the gate. The date taped on. Someone puts a hand on Tom Healy's shoulder when it is necessary to steady him. Healy licks his lips, is red in the face and smiling. Fits himself with a peaked cap and straightens it.

The people around the heifer start to shift on their feet, their pints lowering. Instinctively look back to the doors of the Clarke Martin. A few murmurs and shouts from the turf toss at the other end of the park. Jays John, Keaveney says. Don't you feed your cattle?

The old man tugs on the poncho and they start walking the festival again. The plastic rubbing against itself as the child moves.

There is no way to know what festivals or amusement the child would have known before coming to the old man, if any at all. No one to ask. They pass by the stands with games and sweets and the child does not turn towards them. Is not drawn by the smell of frying meat or the shouts of other children. The old man takes the bun from him and he does not resist.

An ass trots by them, thrashing its head. Reins hanging off it. Leftover from the donkey derby earlier in the day. It sometimes stops to graze on what grass hasn't been matted down by work shoes and runners. Sometimes passes a bystander and the bystander turns to slap its hindquarters, send it jolting along.

Tom Healy's wavering voice rises from somewhere behind the old man and the child. 'S a mháithrín, an ligfidh tú chun aonaigh mé?

Old McGinn slumps behind a small table with a draught board, picking at his nails. Waits for someone to pay two euros to play him. Is known to fall into a coughing fit when losing and bump the table. Next to him the tart raffle, and when the numbers are drawn the old women will gather to see who will take home their baking. Then they'll know to which houses they'll have to call in order to see that it was indeed alright. And McKinney the Ears in the middle with a fistful of tickets, hapless smile.

It is not the yearly pattern festival the town put forth in his youth and the old man wonders if there is a way to tell this to the child. The bravado and swagger of the cattle selling and women lined up to pawn fowl and the offhand matchmaking that went on. The band playing. Soon after the mass the town would start drinking to Our Lady and the more they drank the more they would come up to the old man and tell him what displays of faith and courage he left on the pitch. Struck two and fired over nine from play, and in the thundering rain at that. Put some manners on the county's best, they would say, and they would ask him to do it again the next match. If herself was next to him she would blush at listening to such things. Maybe whisper in his ear to stay gracious, but she would have been pleased to hear all of it.

Two teens waddle through the fair with one welly each, light-stepping with a socked foot. Retrieve their wellies from an open space, return to where they had just stood. Heave them again. It is hard to tell if the contest is sanctioned or initiated by themselves. The teens linger with their hands in their pockets, bump into each other purposely. Appear to get bored. Wind up and fling the wellies at the ass in the middle of the park. The beast continues to graze as the teens' boots land around it.

The old man rests his hand on top of the skull. Taps on it and he and the child start walking again. Finally finish the trek around the grounds. The old man as silent as the child. They come back to the heifer on the painted squares, in time to see Young John fidget. Hear him say, your local farmer is providing you entertainment. So mind yourselves.

Young John forces a playful smile. Pokes at the rump of the heifer. It causes her to swing around, making a few men groan.

Halloran snorts loudly and spits mucous into the grass. Taps two piles of snuff on the side of his hand. Sure, you're big enough to be mostly a manager anyway, he says. Inhales the snuff in one breath. A few laugh, although hesitantly.

Tom Healy stops as he passes them. Shakes his head. Takes off his peaked cap and stuffs it in his back pocket. Turns to one of the men steadying him. Sure Joseph, did you put up the posters?

They watch Tom Healy stagger to the doors of the Stag. Then turn back to the heifer. The heifer swipes at the grass and then remains still, watching something at the other end of the park. Many have dropped their empty pint glasses at their feet.

Halloran shrugs. The wind has carried the smell of your shit to my place often enough, Allen. I suppose I won't miss it this time. Slaps the back of those he passes as he heads towards the pub.

Sure, I've always spread manure on Tawin road, Young John Allen says.

Your shit smells different, Halloran says, walking backwards. As big as you're getting.

What do you mean, Lionel? Young John Allen slips his hands in his pockets. His shoulders lower.

It smells like you're getting notions, John.

Young John looks over to the old man, almost pleading. The old man presses his lips together, lowers his head. Shrugs.

The men standing there watch Halloran cross the street, bow to a pair of old women he passes, then enter the Clarke Martin.

Hey now, I'm helping you out here, Young John yells after him, although he is gone.

The heifer spreads her legs and lifts her tail. Manure slaps the ground on square thirteen, piles, and then splatters.

There you have it, Mulhall says, taking the hat and walking towards the pub himself.

ON THE BOG, BELOW IT

The old man approaches a rock, angled and scraped, hurled from the earth in the bog slide. Sits on it. His footsteps follow the turned ground at the bottom of the hill, bend to where he is. The shape of his wellies deep, as if the old man carries something heavy. He spreads his legs, sticks the hurl into the soil. It stands rigid. The old man looks up the hill and stares into the shimmer of the grey sky.

The bog slide spreads before him. The green and brown slope broke open, turbulent shadows that flume to his feet. The thin trace of a shattered road that lay atop the soil. The dark ground bundled and lurching, like broken furrows toppled over themselves. Cuts a plush boundary with the dried hill grass tangled around it. Water trickling among its relief and pooling in new pools. Car tracks stretch across the slide, band it as if to keep it in place.

The bog, the sky. The old man does not know how long he has looked between them or if he has blinked. Does not know the things he must have thought in the silence. He pulls at his wellies to loose them from the wet ground, resettles himself. Does not trust, at first, that it is the priest toiling on the bog plane above him.

The features of priest, at that distance, merge into the black fabric of his robe and the flesh of his head. His Honda Civic left along the ditch, half-tipped. He moves into the hedge, out of it. Pulls at branches. Bends over the weeds and brush along the edge of the bog. His movements fluid, unheard that far away.

The old man watches. Places a hand on top of the hurl.

The priest traces the hedge's stretch, leans into it sometimes. Then picks up the child's hurl from the grass and reaches into the brush with it. What he gathers he places into a pocket beneath the robe.

The old man blinks. Has maybe looked away. The priest stands at the edge of the bog, staring down at him.

The two of them under a low sky. The bank of dark soil between them. The earth uneven, torn. Heavy with the smell of old clay. Nothing else upright among them, but only themselves. Neither lift a hand in gesture. The priest's robe does not stir at its ends nor does the brush in the hedge around him. The old man breathes and hears only the sound of his breathing.

The priest tosses the sliotar in the air and swings the child's hurl and strikes it. The rap sounds on the bog as the ball lifts higher and into the cloud glare. Dissolves into the sky until it falls again, over the mangled terrain. Lands in front of the old man with a sudden jolt.

The priest stands with his legs spread. All his small movements absorbed by the distance and his contrast against the horizon. The hurl held across his frame.

There is no sun or cloud burst or bird to move across the sky and mark time. That beyond the bog lays unseen from where the old man stands. That around him only soil and the grass and stones scattered through it. He does not look to his footsteps that brought him there. Does not imagine the things he cannot see.

The old man holds his hurl with both hands and stares up. Finally bends and pulls the ball from the earth.

Takes a step forward and swings. Sends the sliotar back to the priest.

MOVING THE COW

The old man lowers the bucket of the tractor over the dead cow. The engine pulses beside the animal. The cow stares into the east with a gel gaze, keeping watch of the horizon. The old man slips the chain over her haunches. Twists it around her rear legs. He raises the arms of the tractor and lifts the backend of 202. Drives towards the dead pile.

Her face slides across the wet grass. The hole in her head deep and vacant. He will notice that she is gone, and that will be something.

THE FISH JUMP

The old man and the child walk the road into town. The child holds a stone, runs it along the wall. Leaves a white scrape through the moss. Winding along.

Pick up your feet, the old man says. The wellies last longer.

The child throws the stone. It bounces in front of them, bounding haphazardly. The old man reaches for the child's hand, but the child doesn't give it. The old man's hurl drags by his feet. When they reach the stone the old man steps over it.

I know you don't mean it, the old man says. He glances to the child, then to the road. Then says, when things happen.

The child pulls up on his trousers. The fabric over his legs straightens and then collapses on the top of his wellies. Does not look at the old man.

Is it something you feel? the old man asks. Well, I know it's how you were made. He lifts his hurl, lets it fall ahead of him, leans on it as he walks. Jarring and such against the world. I know, he says.

A grey Audi comes down the lane, slows before the old man and the child. The woman, grey hair close-cropped. Peers through the glass at the old man, the child. Leaning into the passenger seat. She jams the brake, rocks to a stop.

Two lorries come around the bend, up behind. They honk. She puts the Audi into gear again, looks behind her. Reluctantly drives away. The lettering on the side door flashing.

The old man puts his arm around the child against the strain. They walk silently into town.

The grass along the road heavy with bush crickets. Their buzzing drawl under the grey horizon fills the ears, nose, mouth of the old man. Seems to shake the things around him. Grates on his nerves, tangles them. The child runs along the ditch weeds to silent the insects, but the sound picks up again behind them. Sometimes a bush cricket flings itself in front of them, eventually sinking into the vegetation on the other shoulder. The glaring sound making the air heavy. Settles on their skin. The noise not receding until they reach the concrete perimeter of the town.

The old man holds the door of the Clarke Martin, pushes the child in. The door jangles above. A few at the bar lift their heads, watch him. Nod.

It's that high dollar man, Mulgannon, the cafe owner says. Look after yourself Malachy. He'll buy the pub out from beneath you by the time he's finished his pint.

Malachy sets a stout before him. The old man cups it in his hand as he settles on a stool. The child stands away from him, the other men. Walks along the walls of the pub, head down. Every so often stops and shoves against them, as if he can push them over.

You sure missed one, Malachy, McShane says. The old farmer has the devil in him, sure.

The cafe owner slams down an empty glass. I'll admit it. I didn't mind seeing Young John getting put over the knee and spanked with that hurl. He had it coming, don't you know.

I'm not sure I'd vote for you, Mulgannon, McShane says. But you got a set of bollox hanging off you.

That must be so, Malachy says, taking away the cafe owner's glass. Not just half an hour ago he had a woman asking after him. Well groomed, I'd say. Smelled like the city.

The old man seizes the hurl from his knee and jumps off his stool. Pushes his pint towards McShane. The child circles again and the old man grabs a fistful of the child's shirt and forces him towards the door. Lifts a backward hand in way of leave-taking. The bell clicks over them.

The old man's pint remains on the bar, settling. The cafe owner reaches for it and pulls it closer to him. Well, he says. I guess Mulgannon still has the itch for a woman.

The old man puts his fingers in the eyes of the skull and pulls it along the street. The child is slid ahead in bunches. The humming sound grows, until, leaving the town limits and its traffic murmurs they plunge fully into the droning of the bush crickets. The noise is louder and heavier now. One clings to the old man's shirt, but he leaves it there as he hurries the child along. They pass beneath starlings on an electric line, all looking to where the sun came up although it rose long ago. Tucked into themselves, beads on a string. The old man and the child cross the bridge, and the old man pulls them to a stop. Takes them over the bank.

They weave through the brush, past a pile of manure under a muddle of briar left by 202. Reach the grass edge of the water. They look up to the road, where only the tops of cars glide along the ridge, drifting through whitethorn and sedge. The insect clamour distant and fading.

The old man exhales, slumps. Trudges along the water. He allows the child to follow him at his own resolve.

The dark water is quiet, pushes into itself. Heaving. Their footsteps are kept by the soft grass. Their condensed reflections dragged over the river. The silver flash of a small trout twists over the surface and then plunges.

They don't understand us, the old man says. I suppose it was meant to be like that.

A trout springs into the air, wriggling and turning in the spray before it lands in the grass. Wide-eyed, slick. Its gills flex. Coils over and lies still. Another fish jumps, lands in the briar. Dried chaff clings to its sides. Mouth gaping. Slowly, the stream begins to shatter as the thin slips of fish erupt out of the water, leaping in angles, refracted from somewhere deeper. They fall to the bank soundless and flop among themselves, tangled. The grass below them glistening. Until all that could be heard is the wet beating of the fish on the ground.

The old man takes the child's hand. They walk in silence.

THE
AUCTION

The old man and the child walk through the sale pens hand in hand, the Friesians shifting around them. The cattle with their ears perked, some wide-eyed. Stop chewing when someone comes up behind them, looks them over. Most come to the weekly mart to pass time. The aisles filled with wandering people, clustered. Talking farming and not farming, most of them not farmers. All of the things said buoyant in the smell of cows and sawdust.

The child stops before a cow, traces the ridges of its topline with his fingers. Runs his small hand in the flesh between the ribs. The cow does not stir. The child turns to the old man.

Today men will place a value on her, the old man says. It does not matter what that value will be.

He takes the child's hand again and they walk. The sale shed is not a real shed, does not have clutter, the cracking walls. Is not to one man alone but shared. A hall through which all can amble before the sale. To see the cows that come from other farms, spread like offerings. The old man has not bought a cow in years.

He gets his number at the desk. Did you bring your pocketbook, Mulgannon? the counter assistant asks. The rustle of grease in the canteen behind them. The shouts of kitchen workers. It could have been an innocent jest, but it was not. A few people drinking tea laugh, slumped over chairs, watching him.

The old man folds his number in his back pocket. Takes the hand of the child again.

Young John Allen stands at the other end of the shed. Arms folded over the sales catalogue, glares at the old man. Is not drawing attention to himself because most gazes linger from the old man to the child.

The old man turns from Young John. Says to the child, it's time that you should know. He puts his hands on the child's shoulders. They face the Friesian before them. She reaches back, licks her topline.

It's not so much that there's good cows and bad cows, the old man says. In the end. It's the cows that will last and the ones that don't. It's in the legs. If they stand like a strong cow then it is so.

The old man reaches with his hurl, taps her on the back. She swings to the side, resettles. Then he touches the child's knee with the wood. Says, the cow that stands right will be the last to be culled.

Those in the aisles drift towards the ring, signalling the auction is about to start. People from the town saddled in the wooden stands that surround and hover over the small pen of gates at the bottom. The auctioneer leans on a raised table, overlooking the building and facing the crowd. Scratching notes in the catalogue and rubbing his earlobes between his fingers.

A teenager swings the gate open and the first cow trots into the ring. Throwing sawdust in front of her hooves. A few dealers in vests lean over the pen and rotate their fingers. The people in the stands settle, subdued to only subtle movements as the clerks on either side of the auctioneer scan the audience for bids. The auctioneer chants over the animal in falling then rising figures and broken language. The cow thrashes below him. A few men in the stands raise their hands and the clerks hep and hey to call the bids. The cow is sent out of the ring before the bidding ends so she would grow in the minds of the men pursuing her.

Sold, the auctioneer bellows. Thirteen hundred.

Tommy the Weed leans over to Coughlan. God alive, they paid a fair tune for that one.

The next animal is a two-year-old just freshened. Another youth with a large belt buckle leads her in and removes the halter. She stands broadside, sniffing at the sawdust below her.

Fifteen hundred, the auctioneer shouts, and then becomes his own echo, fifteen, fifteen, fifteen. The clerks hold their hands in front of them, winding them back and forth, searching. Fourteen, fourteen, thirteen.

The chatter in the stands rises as the bid drops to one thousand euros. The cow rubs her chin over the top bar of the gate until the youth pokes at her rump to make her move around the ring. At nine hundred Young John Allen lifts his hand and the clerk yelps to confirm the bid. The auctioneer reaches down to slap at the muzzle of the cow as she tries to lick his papers while he tethers the bidding between Young John Allen and another farmer in the stands, stalled at eleven hundred euros. Once, twice, counts the auctioneer with a raised anvil.

A clerk shouts, Yep!

The building gradually quiets as the crowd follows the clerk's hand to find it pointing to the old man. The old man sits alone with the child in the top corner of the stands. His hurl raised in the air.

The auctioneer hesitates, his breath sweeping over the mike. Then says, eleven-five, eleven-five, eleven-five, twelve, eleven-five.

Young John sits in the front row, the opposite side of the room. His head down, kicking at the sawdust of the ring. Curses silently, aware of the theatre he has found himself in. He lifts his hand.

The old man does too.

The crowd stirs. Reposition their wellies and lean forward. When did Mulgannon get the money to buy anything? Isn't he bust? They make motions with their fingers to suggest that he's as mad as they thought. The cow, picking up on the rising tension, jogs around the ring. Her brisket bouncing off her chest.

Young John nods and another clerk yells, Yep!

The old man lifts his hurl.

Thirteen-five, thirteen-five, thirteen-five. The cow throws her head about her. The plastic tag on her thurl catching the glare of the rafter lights. A crease of sweat on the forehead of the auctioneer as he looks up to watch the men and send his booming voice over the people.

Thirteen-five, Yep!

Fourteen, Yep!

The crowd rocks in their seats. Jays, that's a steep price to pay for that cow. Don't you think? Their heads pulled on the same string held by the clerk, swings them to Young John. Yep! And then to the old man. Yep!

Young John's face reddens. He cannot but look at the old man, the old man sitting motionless. The child beside him, the gaze of the skull wide and undeterred. Young John can walk away and stick the old man with the cow, and that's what winning would be. Under the eyes of the town or not. But still, he raises his hand.

Yep!

The old man lifts his hurl.

The crowd gasps, pulling at each other. Young John jumps off his seat and raises his hands in the air at the old man. Why? he mouths, not sure if the old man can see it or not. Then he bids again.

The old man bids too, bringing the animal to seventeen hundred euros. The auctioneer booms louder, the people tuned taut and bustling. The cow bawls and swings her hind legs in the air. Nearly knocks over the youth as she thrashes by, wild-eyed.

Yes, yells Young John.

The old man raises his hurl.

The clerk offers eighteen-five to Young John and he says, yes, yes.

The old man takes nineteen.

Young John bids twenty.

The old man twenty-one.

Twenty-five, shouts Young John Allen, spit flying from his mouth.

The cow lurches over the gate. Her front hooves clear it but she lands on the top bar—bellowing, and then thrusting into it until the gate collapses and the ring dissolves down to the concrete lip that shapes it. She runs through the first row of seats, bystanders jumping away.

Young John breathes deeply, his shoulders heaving. Hat pulled low over his eyes.

The clerk holds his palm out to the old man. Everyone stares at him. Leans towards him.

The old man lays the hurl on his lap.

The auctioneer counts down the bid. A few teenagers emerge from the hallway of the shed and help the other youth lift the gates. They try to lean them against the concrete. A few men walk calmly towards the cow, the cow stretching her neck below the stands at the feet of the first row. The crowd settles back, people folding their arms with their knees spread, chuckling. Well didn't Mulgannon get him this time. Twenty-five hundred for a cow, that cow! You won't see Young John on the high stool for a while. Tilting their heads, shaking them. Turning to the next animal in the catalogue. The auctioneer takes a swallow of his tea and spits it into the sawdust, readying his voice.

The next heifer to be auctioned is held in the alleyway as a few middle-aged farmers rise from the stands to herd the loose cow. Walk at her with their hands raised. The clatter of conversation lifts and spreads. One clerk slaps the back of the other, and the other wipes his forehead on the front of his shirt and leans on the podium to say something to the auctioneer. The auctioneer reaches over to still the clerk. Points to the front of the ring.

Young John stands in front of the gate. Arms folded, stares up to the stands. The red skin of his neck falling away into his shirt collar. Eyes darting, twitching. He raises a hand, on the edge of words, but says nothing. Rubs his palms on his trousers and trudges away, head down. Then he stops at the edge of the sawdust.

Young John returns to the ring, pulls on the gate, and collapses it again. It crashes against itself. Sawdust billows out in the sweep of air it creates. The sound stills the crowd, clears it of expression in an instant. He looks up into the rows of bystanders looming above him.

I'm only making a living, he says. I didn't choose...

He wrings the end of his shirt in his hands.

Young John looks to the old man, but the old man and the child have already left.

THE BULL IS SHOT

The old man carries calf buckets to the hutches, takes a shortcut through the slatted sheds. His arms spread, rigid, trying not to spill the milk on his trousers. Milk replacer clinging to the hair on his arms, the sweet smell rising off him.

The bull stands in the doorway. Its dark shape against the daylight.

The old man turns behind him. The gate to the bull's pen swung open. The child standing in the crush, watching.

The old man faces the bull again. Sets down his buckets, milk splashing over the side. The bull trots closer, stops.

If it is in you to hit me then you must hit me, the old man says. He looks at the child again, and then closes his eyes.

The bull kicks its legs, bounds ahead. The old man hears it approaching and throwing chaff behind it, feels it, the hot breath, the nearing blow, the force of it charging through the shed, wanting him.

He steps aside.

He hasn't meant to. The bull turns just as suddenly and knocks over the buckets and trips into the gates of the crush. The milk lifts in the air and the bull tumbles forward, the weight thrown against its front leg. The snap of bone echoes between the block walls. The milk falls on the old man and the bull and the bull bellows and writhes on the ground, its eyes wide and rolling.

Ryan Dennis

The old man wipes the calf milk off his forehead. He stands over the bull.

The bull lays its chin on its barrel, its head rising and sinking with the swell of its breath, and then lifts it to bawl again. The animal prostrate before the old man. The old man reflected in its eyes, small and distorted, cast against the dimming grey.

The child is still in the crush. He lunges at the child and the child does not flinch as the old man grabs him and drags him over the concrete. Bursts through the doors of the dairy. The doors snap behind them. He throws the top off the empty bulk tank, lowers the child inside.

He shuts the lid and walks away.

The old man does not like to look at the bull but he knows that he must. It has settled, its ears drooping over its broad cheeks. A low moan rising from deep inside it. The leg at an odd angle, the rigid edge of bone pushed against the skin.

It laying at his boots, pained and resigned, he wants to tell it things. Not just that he respected it and is sorry for it, but all the things the old man has never said out loud before. To give it comfort, if it were in the old man to give comfort. To lament or eulogise. Instead he raises the hurl in the air and looks the bull in the eye. The wood edge shaking, teetering in his hands.

He lets the hurl fall to his side. Leans it against the wall. Goes to the dairy.

The child is standing beneath the latch when he opens it. His skin already cool and damp. His breath echoing. The old man grabs the front of his shirt and lifts him out.

He places the child in front of the wincing animal and leaves and returns with a rifle. He puts the rifle in the child's hands and then bends down to him.

It was in his nature to do this, he yells at the child. He sticks his finger in the child's chest, pushing him back. Through gritted teeth he says, he didn't know any better. This is what happens when you let him do as he does.

The old man cocks the lever and walks away. In the back of

the head, he says without turning around. The front will do no good. Two if you have to.

OPPORTUNITY FOR PARTING

The Ford ambles down the lane, low gear. The turf trailer on back, humming behind it. The ash turned to sludge on the road, the wet rubber peeling over it. Two parallel lines follow after the tailgate. The child sits in the trailer, cross-legged. The floss lifts up, stirs behind it.

The ash settled over the rocks in the wall, dulling the colour of the lichen, bunching in the gaps between stones. Feathering the hedge. The lane a dull-skinned channel the tractor passes through, the blank sky a top to it. Where one starts and the other ends is difficult to tell with the pale land. Or the sky has come down upon them at last, to smother them. Press out the things living. The tractor nears the entrance to the bog, the scars of burnt ground swaddled in grey down. The tractor slows. And then passes the bog.

The tractor lowers in pitch, rolls to a stop at the end of the lane. The old man sits behind the window a long time. A steely film over it, filtering his image. He doesn't meet his own eyes. Finally exhales, gets out. Lifts the child out of the back and takes his hurl from behind the seat.

They cross into the East Field at the end of his property, hand in hand. The stretch before them colourless, pristine. Trees and fence lines and the things that rise from the ground soften together, fold in. The world before them sullen. Cracked only by the footsteps behind them.

When they reach the end of the field they stop. The old man looks down. Then points.

Keep walking that way. At some point you'll find people. Eventually one of those people will take you in.

The old man and the child stare into the sallow distance. The old man's breath the only thing audible. Its slight rise. The child does not look up. A rook crosses in front of them, a dark centre point drifting. Does not land in the breadth of their vision but disappears. The world before them again a single note, sustained. The old man exhales.

Alright then. Let's go.

He takes the child's hand and they turn around. Their footsteps cut through the ash in an arc. Meet up at the end of the field.

THE MATCH

Drizzle from the sky and the grass slips greasily. Yields under the wellies of the old man and child as they near the pitch. The match already started. The town's halfback trails an opponent down the side-line on his way to kick it over the bar. Two sets of stands and people huddled on them, like flesh over ribs. Their knees up, arms folded. The old man leads the child to the fence, where they stand apart.

Drive it, shouts Farrar from the stands. Drive it, drive it, God damn you. The team sends it far wide of the post, the ball rolling off the pitch. A youth is sent to retrieve it from the car park. They're wretched, the lot of them, Gill whispers to Lonegan. They'll come around, they'll come around, Lonegan says, mostly to himself. They watch the old man, the child. The crowd sits sedated in the rain. Clapping their hands time to time without realizing it.

The old man leans his hurl against the fence, folds his arms over the top rail. If he turns around at any point he will find people staring at him, but he does not turn. The crowd bunched, knitted together. Making whispers and glances. I'd be surprised if he's looking after the little bullock properly, don't you think? Does he go to school even? You don't suppose Mulgannon... One of their cornerbacks picks up a miskicked ball and sends it up the pitch, and the old man taps the fence in recognition. The old man offers to lift the child up, but the child puts his head against the chain link. Presses into it.

The next time the old man looks down it is no longer only him, the child, at the fence. Another small boy and girl linger nearby. The girl holding her dress in her fist and swinging her arms side to side. The other boy pushes his hand down the back of his pants, itches absently. The child stands before them, the rust of the chain links on the wet bone.

The old man does not recognize the children. Looks to the stands. He tries to smile at them but then swallows and spits. Heya, he says, and because he cannot think of anything else to say, he says it again.

The girl, the boy, stand motionless before the child, engrossed by the skull. The girl tilts her head. The boy rocks. Staring.

The child blows on them.

First on the girl, leaning forward, his cheeks welling with air that is released in a long rustling whisper. He doesn't seem to take a breath as he turns to the boy and blows over him. The boy and girl's heads lifting, drawn up, wide-eyed. They titter and sway and pull at each other.

Suddenly, the girl is wrenched backwards by the hands of her mother. Her fingers a tight grip on the girl's arms. The woman signals back to the stands with the jerk of her head, causing a man to rise from his seat and stumble through the people below him.

Íosac, the woman says.

Brown hair, jeans. He nods. Does not know her. The crowd applauds as one of their own puts it over the bar.

I'm real sorry there, Róisín bothering ye. She tucks the girl behind her legs.

He doesn't get bothered, the old man says. The woman doesn't know how to respond, if it is a joke or not. She exhales when the man from the crowd arrives and stands by his son.

Mulgannon, the man says, reaching out his hand. Then says, sure, listen. He looks to the woman. The formality of their glances suggesting they are not together. It's nothing against you. He glimpses down at the child out of the corner of his eye, and then realizing that he did so, says, or him, certainly.

And if they wanted to hang around the farm, all things considered, the woman says. You never know when they wouldn't know any better, and the danger of it.

Bit out of place here, no? the man says. He looks at the pitch in the silence that follows. Then the man jolts. The hurley, the hurley! I mean, at a football match. His hands swing about him, then settle in his pockets. You were quite the stormer with it. My old lad told me. I mean, back when they played it here proper.

Life is hard enough as it is, and we just want them to be safe, the mother says.

The crowd cheers again. One of the town's forwards has put it in the net. The scoreboard shows the team only down by three points, two minutes before the half.

The child continues to blow towards the boy and the girl, turning his body to face them as they stand by the legs of their parents. Blows a little harder. The boy and girl fixed on him.

Then the man says, look. We know it's not right in the general sense. He reddens. Still holds his hands out, as if there is something in them to offer.

The woman gasps. The girl has stepped out from her legs and struck the child.

The child flinches. Then leans forward and blows on her. She balls her small fist up, lifts it, and swings stiffly again. It strikes the skull, jarring it uneven. The man moves towards her but stops, glancing at her mother, allowing space for his son to run up and hit the child too. Giggling. The child leans and blows over him.

The woman lunges towards her daughter but stops short. The hurl is raised in front of her. They are playing, the old man says. I think so. Yes, they are playing.

The father reaches for his son. The old man steps before him. Let them play.

The girl and boy clout the child. Taking turns, laughing. On his body, his head. The girl hits him in the cheek bone, rocking him backwards. It deflates his mouth as he gathers himself. She shrieks and puts her hand to her eyes. The boy stomps on the toes of the child, swinging his arms wildly.

Róisín! the mother hisses. She motions for her daughter to come but the girl will not turn to her.

The father yells to his son. Slaps his thigh in anger. Then pleads to his son to stop. The child's face is red, his eyes squinting. His blowing raspy, laboured.

They are playing, the old man says. As children do.

The town's centre-half spins around the last back and lamps the ball past the stretched arms of the goalie. It ties the score as the final seconds of the half expire. The spectators rise to their feet and shout, whistling and clapping as their team trots off the field. The cheers of the town drown out the howl of the mother reaching for her daughter. She calls her daughter's name and charges towards her, but abruptly recoils as her chest collides into a weathered hurl held in front of her. The old man stands with his legs spread apart and when the father, unsure, stretches towards the children the old man swings at him. The mother bawls. She tries to push her way to her daughter, the old man leaning back against her weight, her arms straining past the shaft of the hurl, her panicked screams lost in the hailing crowd.

Gill shoves through the people on their feet in the stands. Grabs Lonegan's knee for balance as he edges by him. Past Farrar.

Where you going? Lonegan asks. We might win this one.

Gill laughs. I'd rather leave thinking we did than give it a chance to know otherwise.

Lonegan watches him step onto the grass. Finally shrugs and follows after him. Farrar sits on the planks slumped, until Lonegan reaches through the people and taps his elbow. Then he sighs and rises too.

FIRE ON THE BOG

The old man stares into the darkness. Calls out to the child.

The footsteps of the child in the spreading night. Circling the old man, the old man pitches turf. After the evening milking because he likes being on the bog at this time, when all is black and there is no distinction between what is sky and what is not and even the bending ground, because it is not solid, is already dissolving into the thing above it. So the old man thinks. And the darkness not a thing he is between, but an inseparable part of. He calls the child again and sees his shadow pass before him.

The turf he lifts from the ground, the stacks, like carcasses of once violent things. Heaves them into the trailer. Over the ditch grass rising up. Traces his path to the next stack.

Go not far, the old man calls out, and then says, things lurk. He thinks he hears the child rustling the uncut ground. What things, he cannot tell the child. Not because the old man has not stood on the same ground and looked into the darkness for all the time before. But because he suspects the things that stir unseen are different now. He is not sure how to name them, or if they have skin to grasp.

Don't tarry, Child, he says. To help would be better. He takes measured steps, the turf in his arms. Moves from bog to trailer and back like a jolting pendulum, making bare the ground, as if clearing the land of monuments and the stories they held. Pull against me world, he thinks.

A bit of sweat on his temple cooling in the night. Because it is night and not the waking day the old man thinks he can be good to himself. Sits down for a moment, on the bucket he takes from the tractor hitch. No sooner sits down then stands up and brings the bucket to the tractor. He takes the rubber hose from the back of the seat, siphons diesel from the machine, uses it to light a stack of turf. Hovers by it.

He sits for a second, then stands again. Child, he calls out. He paces the fire. The moisture on his wellies glares in the low light. The matted ground around it dense, fibrous. He makes a tight orbit. Muted flames reaching for his trouser legs. In the small light of the dark open he sees parts of himself, and it grieves him.

He keeps pacing. Lifts one wellie then another, faint ground-whispers beneath his soles. Paces, his body dropping into rhythm. His arms swing further from him. Turning around the fire, in even tempo, straight-gaited. His head tilts towards the flame. Pulled in.

That's the hell of it, isn't it? he thinks. The thing a man is up against can't be shook, struck. Notions that mean to harm. Not a man or a band of men you can stand in front of but things that come out of the shadows. Could be here now, he thinks. Not sure if he said it out loud.

Child! he shouts, but does not stop turning about the fire to listen. He was always on the defensive, wasn't he? Always the one taking it. He brushes his hand along the top of the flames and feels them reach for him. That's the way of it, isn't it? Sure, that's the way of it.

He steps through the fire. The burning push inside him rushing out to meet the flame. Walks towards the tractor. Chi-ild! he yells in two parts. He sticks the hose in the diesel tank. It bends when it hits the bottom. He draws hard on it, the malevolent rush into his mouth. Fills his senses. Wonders if he'll burst into flame himself. Fills the bucket.

He walks along the rows of turf, tipping the bucket. The smell of diesel swelling over the ground. Blue paper towels used for milking stick out of his back pocket. He rolls and lights them. Holding the burning torch in his hand, lifts it. Then peels off a disappearing layer and drops it onto a stack. The turf takes flame. He unsheathes another writhing sheet. Drops it.

The bog alight. Flames rising from the soft ground. Each stack a station of flame. Like a rite to summon heinous spirits. The old man spreads his legs and stands among it. Come now, he says to the darkness around him. See what I have done.

Smoke curls above the stacks, pools above the old man's head. Dark strings of a darker harp. He's outside it. Feels the heat anchor into his skin. Tug. The lifting musk of burning turf. The old man hears voices. Turns about himself. Wonders if they are inside him. Child?

He steps into the fire.

The air like hot grease. Settles inside him. The voices grow, tangle among themselves. Chaff floats by him in the haze, glimmer like shards of a mirror. Shape-sounds on the edge of words, the voices. Child, he whispers. The crackling of the fire or the breaking of bones, among it he hears footsteps he thinks. They've come around at last. Have come to take form. A silhouette stands behind the curtain of heat. A flame flickering through it.

The heat presses in on him. Draws things from him. He kicks over the burning stack at his feet. Crushes the colour of glowing turf beneath it. Embers' last light pushing through the bottom of his wellie. Makes space for himself on the ashen ground. Mulgannon, the darkness shouts.

He stops. Peers out through the flames.

Mulgannon, come out now.

The face of Whelan emerges in the haze, recedes in it. The shadows of beasts pull apart into the shapes of humans. Another face, disembodied, then gone.

The ground below the old man steams. Hisses below his

heels. His cheeks glisten. The front of his shirt hangs low, heavy with sweat. The clatter outside the fire grows. Words lifting into the dark void. The old man's name twisted among them.

The landscaper steps into the fire. Or his likeness. He says, Íosac, will you come out? He slaps at his skin and draws into the abyss.

Do they have the child? the old man wonders. Is that why they are trying to tempt him? Dark soot collects on the burnt hairs of the old man's arm. His hair wet and grating on his skull. He tries to call for the child but his voice scrapes inside him. Child? he whispers.

A hand reaches in, open-palmed. Fingers brushing along the old man's jumper and disappears. Flames intertwining in front of him. The old man backs up. The breath of the night heavy on his neck.

The child stands behind him. Against the back wall of flame, the shifting gleam. His sleeves drooping over his knuckles. The crawling fire reflected on the glare of the skull. The old man grabs him by the front of his shirt and pulls him to the middle. He stands in front of the child, still grasping him. Dried stalks of bog weed drift between them.

Mulgannon, Mulgannon, Mulgannon his name lifts around him, bent and mangled in the flame, the whirr of voices interlocking, pulling in. There are more and then more. The demons gathering. Mulgannon would you just come out? Mulgannon. Jesus, the boy's there too!

The boy, oh my god the boy, they shriek. Baying, frenzied. The boy, the boy. It's not right. Is he not in trouble? Jesus the boy.

The old man steadies himself. Looks into the smoke. Clasps the child.

Young John Allen emerges from the haze. Íosac. Be easy now. Íosac. Takes off his John Deere hat and wipes it over his forehead. In his balled fist. His arms open, inching towards the old man. Give me the child, he says. Give him to me now.

You will not, the old man whispers.

Íosac, listen to me.

The old man leans forward, sweat in his eyes. He's what I have.

Give him to me Íosac.

I won't.

The fluttering apparition of Young John Allen lunges past the old man towards the child. The old man heat-heavy, dazed, does not blink until Young John drags the child through the careening fire in front of them. The old man grunts. Tilts his head back and takes a gasping breath and then lurches blindly into the flames at the disappearing figure of Young John Allen and then driving into the solid hull of the fiend itself, the mass of them joined, collapsing to the ground. The old man's wellies plunge through a turf stack and rains shattered fire upon them. Mulgannon, the demonhead whispers in its folded breath.

The child stands next to them, looking down. Behind him gather the townspeople. A suspension of faces held in the haze, floating around them. Tilting their heads, peering.

The old man clutches the ankle of the child and lifts the other fist at them. Cinders rising from the bog, fading to darkness. What he thought was embers he now sees as the burning eyes of a dog, black as the darkness around it. Lurking on the edge of the cut ground. Creeping closer.

GEIR SULLIVAN TIPPED OVER

Two pigeons land in a grass patch in the lane. Bob their heads, turn about themselves. Scatter as Geir Sullivan's lorry turns the corner. Tyres throwing loose gravel behind them.

He leans back. Forearm over the steering wheel, fingers bending to a fist. Music plays, but Geir, slumping, does not react to the tinny rhythms from the stereo. Slows down in front of the farm of Íosac Mulgannon.

He rolls down the window, the glass scraping as it draws in. Puts his other arm out of it. Looks at the old grey place. There are cracks in the shed wall like thin arteries. Clutter of rusting machinery. All familiar to Geir Sullivan by now. A page he stares at but doesn't read. All signs of crazy. His mother used to say that you can't reason with crazy. You can only wait it out.

The old man explodes from behind a hedge in the Ford.

Geir Sullivan jerks his arm inside and grips the wheel. He tries to veer left but the lorry glances off the lane wall. Stones topple behind him. Before he can speed away the old man is upon him, the bucket poised and then pushing into the frame. The old man's face burns red and the thin hair on his head sprung taut. He is feral-eyed and grinning.

The bucket thrusts into the undercarriage and Geir is wrenched sideways inside the cab. The tractor's arms lower, the back wheels spinning. The loader works itself under the

141

lorry, wedging beneath its steel. The vehicle tipping. Geir shouting Hey! Hey! Hey! He pushes on the passenger door but gravity thrusts it shut again. He puts his arms around the steering column, head on the wheel, shrieks. The tractor strains, creaks brazenly, as it lifts the lorry up and drops it on the other side of the wall.

The old man backs up slowly. He parks the tractor in the driveway, pulls out the stopper. Starts the heifer chores.

THE SKY
FALLS

Rye chaff slides down the rattling windscreen, dragging dust
with it. Through the image of the hedgerow in front of it. The
head and then the torso of Eoin the Wood push through
the brush. He steps out, shakes his legs from the grasp of
the whitethorn. Rubs the marks on his neck and looks into
the hedge. Coleman thrusts through a snarl of low hanging
branches, flinches as they bend off his chest. The men's
features blurred by the twitching glass. By the time they make
their way towards the tractor Mary Flaherty has reached
the meadows too, scurrying after them in short, stiff strides.
They heave into the uncut grass, a phantom trail of bent stalks
behind them.

The child remains tucked by the steering column. The old
man rubs the back of his knuckles on the window. Places his
hand on top of the skull. Leaves the grey shape of his fingers
on the bone.

Starlings land at the far end of the field, a dark mass
plunging to the ground to pick at the exposed grass stems.
They twist among each other in rigid movements, collide into
each other's paths and flutter. One takes flight and the others
lift up as well, turn through the sky.

The old man reaches the end of the row and then raises the
hay head and turns the tractor on the headlands. It pauses,
idles. The old man rubs his fingers along the gauges on the

dashboard, checks the engine temperature, pressure. Picks an empty McVities package off the floor, balls it up, and puts it behind the seat. Then starts back into the field where the townspeople stand, the cutter bars static.

The Ford eases to a halt. Everyone stares at the silhouette of the old man behind the door. Tipped forward, still. The bonnet of the tractor rocks. Heat from its ribs brindles the air, distorting the horizon behind it. Coleman steps back when the hot air reaches his face. The door opens.

You will not, he says from the seat of the tractor. Then slowly climbs out, holding the grab bar. The hurl. The rapping of the Ford's engine is loud and Eoin the Wood has to yell to be heard, turning red in the face. Would you see us all dead first, Íosac? he says.

Mary Flaherty steps into the windrow the discbine has just made, watches the insects it has stirred. Finally says, Eoin, be kind.

The child sits with his knees to his chest. His features indistinguishable behind the dusty glass. Only the shadow-holes of the skull's eyes seen shifting.

Eoin the Wood looks to Coleman, but Coleman keeps his head down. Snaps the rye bristle beneath his shoes as he shifts his weight.

Eoin the Wood gathers mucous in his throat and spits into the hay. Throws his arms up.

The child climbs into the tractor seat, faces out the back. On his knees. Puts his small hands on the window. A muted click echoes inside the cab as the child leans forward and the skull hits the glass.

The old man raises the hurl to his waist, gripping both ends of the shaft. The machine pulses below him.

Eoin, Mary Flaherty says. She touches his shoulder but he shrugs off her hand.

If you won't send him away then we will, Eoin the Wood says. Mulgannon, give us the child.

Wood, says Coleman.

Eoin the Wood picks up a stone, throws it at the tractor. It bounces off the back window with a dull knock and lands in a windrow. Lays atop the grass. Give us the child, Mulgannon.

Eoin the Wood starts towards the tractor.

The old man lifts his hurl violently in the air, holding it, shaking.

Scratches a split in the sky.

Mary Flaherty looks up. The piece of ash circles as it falls. Because the sky itself is a slate-cast void and the distance from which it presses down cannot be marked, the falling thing may have been as destructive and jarring as a meteor meant to extinguish them, or only a piece of cloud shredded from above. The other people in the field follow the path of Mary Flaherty's gaze until they, too, are watching it fall. They quiet and still, their eyes following it in unison.

It lands in Coleman's hair.

Eoin the Wood plucks it off the fabric. It turns to dust in his fingers.

The sky crumbles as it releases the grey drift. It floats to the earth, on trousers and shoelaces and the blades of meadow grass around them. Snow had fallen twice last year, but now no one gathers up the ash in their hands or stand with their mouths open and head thrown back, hoping to catch some of it on their tongues. They brush it off their arms, but that only rubs it into their clothing. Futile against the silent assault.

Standing in the open field, the townspeople draw closer. Coleman holds his jumper over himself and Mary Flaherty, their heads lowered. Eoin the Wood lifts an open palm in front of him, watching it gather over his fingers. His face has turned pale and he does not look towards the tractor. The child stands on the steps, the ash pooling and sometimes sliding down the curve of the skull. It fills in the angles of the bone and further conceals the child's expression.

The old man lowers his hurl, shields his eyes with his

fingers and gazes up. The ash clings to the chaff on the hay head, grows. Gets caught in dried dirt on the Ford's bonnet. The cut and uncut ground fading together. Let's go, Eoin the Wood says and pulls on Coleman. Coleman shakes the ash off his jacket and into the grass, where it lays over the top of the stems. They walk past the old man on the steps of the tractor, avoiding his eyes. Mary Flaherty stands dazed, stares after them. She finally leaves too. The windrows shaken into green colour again as the townspeople cross them.

The ash does not stop. There is no wind to stir it or take it away, nor rain in all the time that it falls. The river grows heavy, thickens as it dissolves onto its surface and is slowly pushed between stones. It falls on the town and the fields around it, on the roads that lead between them. It bunches on the roofs of shops, bleeding out the print on their signs. On the fences that keep livestock. The shape of paddocks lost as they blend into the hedgerows around them. The cows are held in sheds, but often stand in the doorway, ash collecting on their necks.

The next day it is explained that a volcano has erupted in Iceland and that an air current has brought the ash in a bundle and dumped it over the town. The people of the town, not knowing what to do, carry on as they have before. Customers shake at the loose folds of their clothing in front of the glass door of the SuperValu. School children turn from their lessons to watch the silt collect on the windowsills. Old Henry McBride still slumps underneath the awnings of Kelly's with his arms folded as he always has, the ash settling on him and turning him into the leaden shape of himself. The town, with its buildings and benches and trees, is covered in the ash and soon only a silhouette, a shadow of what it was before.

The fields, at first, surge under the thin dusting, spurred by the new fertilizer. By the second day, however, if the grey down is kicked away there is the grass yellowing and withering beneath it. A few cars drive by the farm slowly, watch the child walk across the lawn, crossing over his tracks in the drift and kicking it up in front of him. Rolling around in it until he is grey himself. There is a worry among them that perhaps the ash will not stop and they will be buried beneath it, daily living becoming abbreviated beneath its weight, until it grows heavy enough to still everyone, muffling all shouts and fidgeting.

It soon stifles the town. Many become as quiet as the ash that falls. Some, like the cattle, stand behind their kitchen windows and look up to the sky for hours, silent. They rub at their necks and shoulders, suddenly realizing the ache, made further forlorn because whatever they imagined to be up there is now flaking away and will not stop until there is only a shapeless gap above.

Before long the sky and the ground match, a grey emptiness without colour or detail, stretching in endless distance. A man can walk the lane with the feeling that all he had thought was around him does not exist and never has, that it is only him, and the choices he has made. But where he would go to account for those choices he does not know.

On the third day it begins to rain. At first the solitary drops fall with soundless impact into the ash over the ground, but then the ash begins to shiver and hiss, finally dissolving into a pale sludge that seals the earth. It clings to the boots of children that walk to school and the windscreens of cars. Most have to pull off the road every few miles and wipe the glass off with their jumpers. It settles between the clefts of the stone walls and over the church bell as it swings. Frogs leave prints in the paste as they cross the boreens. It is tracked into households and onto kitchen floors. When the room is heated by the range a sulphurous tinge rises between the walls. The people themselves have it in their clothing and caked in the hair on their arms and often have it smudged on their faces, no one bothering to point it out anymore.

READING

The old man takes the book off the dresser. Rusty bolts shift below his hand. The child lies next to him in the dark. His small chest rising silently. The old man's jumper he milked in lays on the floor, its thin arms stretching, twisting. His trousers crumpled, smelling of manure. The old man reads.

It is then that they approached Cúchulainn, and his sword was upright in his hand and he gripped it tight as he died, and none of the men of Ireland could release the sword from him.

The old man puts the book down. Presses his fingers over his eyes. Starts to cry anyway.

COLLECTING RUBBISH

Eoin the Wood holds a used condom in front of him. There you have it, he says. I do declare the old ways dead.

He walks it over to the lorry on the side of the road, drops it into a rubbish bag held by Farrar. Farrar sits off the tailgate, the bag withered and stretched between his legs. Stares off into the distance. The old man's discbine cuts a meadow at the end of the road, bottom of the valley. Crawling under a slate sky.

It's lovely you fellows being here today, Mary Flaherty says. Good for community spirit, is it not? She pours tea from a thermos to paper cups. Puts them on the bonnet of the lorry. Nods to them whenever someone looks up.

The volunteers spread across the roadside, kicking through the ditchgrass, leaning over the wall to catch any metallic gleam in the weeds. The priest throws a shredded tyre over the back of his neck, whistles an old hymn as he crouches again. Coleman picks up a beer can and the shattered pieces of a vehicle's grill. Takes them to Farrar's bag. Farrar picks the can out again, shakes it, then drops it back in. Lonegan holds up a dead squirrel. Tosses it in.

Maybe we'll win this year, Mary Flaherty says.

O'Farrell takes a stray flier, wraps it around a Lucozade bottle filled with urine, carries it gingerly. Tidy Town to fuck, he says.

The old man's discbine grows in pitch as it nears the closest headlands, then recedes as it starts down the other side of the field.

O'Farrell overlaps the others bent over the shoulder, swinging back and forth with stooped heads. The townspeople mumbling to one another as they matt down the vegetation with their runners. Eoin the Wood slides into the seat of the lorry, stares vacantly though the windscreen and waits for Mary Flaherty to remove the tea from the bonnet. He drives the lorry ahead, Farrar hanging out the back.

Instead of getting out Eoin the Wood remains in the seat, his arm hanging over the steering wheel. Then opens the back window. Leans towards it but doesn't take his eyes from the old man's mower.

Ye lads were farmers, weren't ye?

Farrar grunts. Doesn't bother turning around.

The townspeople along the road start to look up. Fidget with the rubbish they hold.

The priest puts his head down, spreads his large palms over the cloth on his stomach. Exhales. Searches for his tobacco in his robe.

Eoin the Wood gets out of the lorry. Shuts the door gently so as not to disturb the paper cups of tea Mary Flaherty has set back on the bonnet. You're friends and all, he says, jerking his head at Lonegan. But how do you put stock into someone who's crazy?

Crazy, crazy, Farrar says. Steady on, Wood.

A few more people empty their hands into Farrar's bag, even if only holding a stray bolt or a Cadbury wrapper. Just to linger by the lorry.

Lonegan kicks at the tyre, stares after the old man's discbine.

More townspeople collect by the tailgate, lean on its bed, its hubs. Arms hanging over the lip. Farrar starts to shift uncomfortably. Surrounded.

Collins says, that old way of farming. Then says, sure what

do I know. If you could change time itself, then sure.

Sure who knows what he's liable to do? the seamstress says. He's a danger. Look at the boy.

The boy, Duffy says.

Please, says Mary Flaherty. Come on, now. We have the Tidy Town in just one week. She takes the thermos and fills the cups on the bonnet even fuller. Says, there's milk of course.

The mention of the child stills the townspeople. Causes some to fold their arms across their chests. Their small movements drawing them closer together. Condensing. The priest continues to kick his foot through the ditch weeds. His head down.

We should have left Mulgannon in that fire, the seamstress says. Would have sorted itself out.

Was it the child that set the turf on fire? asks Coleman. Playing and the like?

Ah, there's something right off about that boy. You know it yourselves, Fitzpatrick says.

The old man's discbine lowers in pitch as its cutter bars still and it swings on the headlands, turns and starts another windrow. The old man and the child not visible in the Ford at that distance. The machine's drawl settling over the townspeople.

We can't have anyone wasting our turf, Eoin the Wood says. He slaps the lorry. Turns to the priest. Says, you've done right by us before in these matters. We'd be grateful.

Would you talk to him? Coleman says. Tell him to send the boy away. You're the priest, after all. Our priest.

The priest lifts up a rusted bumper, tucks it under his arm. Bends to pick up the shattered Buckfast bottle, the pieces clinking against each other as he drops them into one of his palms. Grabs a crisp bag out of a strand of cattails by pulling it through the rigid stalks. Runs his foot along the dusty grass on the shoulder, even though his hands are full.

He returns to the back of the truck, his eyes lowered, and

empties his arms into the black rubbish bag. Wipes his hands on his soutane.

The priest starts back to the side of the road. His thick hands in fists at his side. Turns back to the people gathered at the truck. The boy, he says. The flesh on his head colouring. Wouldn't we lose the best part of ourselves?

The seamstress steps forward and points a finger at him. I knew you were weak.

The priest holds up his hands, maybe out of habit. Curses under his breath and then shakes his head. Íosac has conviction, he says. More than any of us. Does it matter in what?

How much of ourselves, of our town, do we have to give for the sake of the child? Coleman asks.

Your decency, the priest says.

Eoin the Wood starts pacing in front of the lorry. Shakes his head. Puts his hands in his pockets and then takes them out and slaps the lorry's bonnet. Well, the turf, he says. Then he pulls up his belt and starts towards the adjoining meadows. His movement slowed by the hay against his trousers. Lunges into the hedgerows beyond it. The other townspeople gather where Eoin the Wood has just stood and stare after him. Look to each other. Coleman eventually shrugs. Follows after him in a laboured jog.

Mary Flaherty sets her cup of tea down. Carefully weaves through the people to be able to see both Eoin the Wood, Mulgannon's tractor. Grabs her elbows and says, ah Íosac. Then lifts up her dress and hurries towards them.

SPREADING SLURRY

The old man lowers himself to his knees, lifts on the planks over the slurry grate by the heifer shed. Pulls a handkerchief from his back pocket, presses it over his nose, mouth, leans in. Peers into the abyss and waits for the strata of shadow to sift out what in the darkness is manure and what is not. His eyes water. He rocks back onto his heels and stares into the paste-grey sky. It has been still for days, without anything from it to stir a blade of grass. He stares at it a long time, his head cocked back, until he gets dizzy. Is this the way it is then? he asks.

He rises unsteadily and hooks onto the slurry tank.

The heifers run back and forth along the fence line. Stopping to pull at a mouthful of grass before kicking up their rear legs and running again. He had moved them out of the shed before spreading because of the methane that rises from the stored slurry. First time on pasture, behind a wire, their dirty hooves running through the coarse grass. The old man leans beside the agitator. It shakes his body, stirring all the looseness out of it. When the tank is full he disconnects the pipe, stuffs the handkerchief into his back pocket, and climbs into the tractor.

The weight of the manure pulls on the Ford, pushes into it when he stops at the end of the driveway. The tank borrowed and expected back tomorrow. The tractor bouncing along the lane, between the stone walls. Turns into a field.

The old man starts in the corner of the field and pulls a lever and then pushes on the PTO. The tractor vibrates with fever pitch and sends a storm cloud of manure behind the tank that the old man governs. It drums on the grass, leaving behind its wet shade. The dark smell of slurry fills the tractor cab. There is a simple pattern to work like this that his body falls into. The first trip around the field his mind takes it in, its shape and hazards, and is freer to separate, disassociate as he makes more turns on the headlands. There is a certain part of the day, between the beginning of doing something and when he becomes worn by doing it over and over that the old man begins to dislodge from the soreness of the world, the demand of it. Feels like, he thinks, how he is meant to feel.

When he pulls back into the driveway he must stop short for the heifer racing in front of him, thrashing its head. The fence wire lays flaccid in the grass. Never being behind a fence they did not know to respect it, had run through it or pushed on it until it collapsed. Now they frolic between the shed and the house, tearing at the lawn grass. He will get them later.

The old man connects the agitator pipe to the slurry spreader and turns it on. The cylinder shakes with the manure that pulses through it. He bunches the handkerchief on his hand and presses it on his face. Bends over to look into the grate. Takes the fabric away just to spit into it and listen to its depth. As he pulls away in the Ford some heifers follow after him, bawling.

In the field a hooded crow lifts itself to flight before the tractor. Its sloppy wings like a heavy cloth, settling out of his path. It turns its head to watch him. The brush in the hedgerow still. He nearly resents the calm. The respite. Because it is not so with the child. Everything lies in wait. The old man wishes it would instead show itself. Allow him to push against it.

He empties the slurry into the field. Feels the ease of the tractor relieved, like he would in his own body. The grass bent with the dark weight. The grass grows better because of the shit placed on it. He refuses to see meaning in it. And then laughs because he has made that decision. His throat getting sore.

The heifers cluster before the gate at the road and scatter before the machine as he turns in. He tries to tie the handkerchief around his face as the tank rocks on its tyres, filling. But his fingers fumble behind his head. Hello, he shouts into the grate. Devil, are you in there? His eyes water and his body sways as he climbs the steps of the tractor. Yee-haw! he yells out the window to the heifers, but the engine muffles the sound.

The tank heaves along the ground as the tractor pulls it to where the last pass has trailed off. He turns on the PTO without slowing. Old Miss Molly, bird full of folly, he sings. The number of loads he takes out will be a number he sleeps with tonight. A companion. To empty the damn thing would be better, sure. The skin on his face burns, from the inside. He opens the tractor door for more air but the tractor jostles over the earth and the door swings shut on its own. Finally the world shows itself, the old man thinks. Wants to fight back. Old Miss Molly, hole full of snolly.

Comes to a slamming stop in front of the agitator. Leaves the tractor door open as he lowers down the steps. What's the craic, Boy? he yells into the grate, on his hands and knees. His echo rises back to him. Who lives chained in the abyss? Come out already and let me beat you.

He climbs back into the tractor. The handkerchief lying on the ground. Clay leaps behind the tyres. Mudded tread pressed into the surface of the lane. The old man can hardly see for the tears in his eyes, dust on the windows. Turns into the field and releases the manure, a jagged path across the grass. Turns at the hedgerow. He opens the door again and stands on the steps. Come! he shouts, the tractor bouncing along the field. He clutches the grab bar and leans away from the motor. Come!

The old man beats his head against the agitator pipe as it fills and shakes and fills the tank. Turns it off. Then kicks the pipe away with the heel of his wellie. The heifers stand before him, ears perked. He runs after them, his elbows flailing. Screaming. They dart away and settle and he falls as he turns. His body aflame. Screams, gets up and chases after them.

The child stands in the doorway of the shed, watching.

The tractor jerks out of the driveway, throwing the old man into the seat. Everything around him shaking, the belly laugh of a fiend. He turns liquid. Disappears, reappears. Stand, stand, he whispers to himself. The tractor, tank, scrapes against the right wall. Turns the stones to dust, leaves them in piles. He lifts his hand in front of him, lets his fingers collapse on the steering wheel. Brushes against the left wall. The tank swinging, colliding. The impact passes through the old man. Awakens him, turns him to stone. The tractor veers sideways and hits the wall head on.

The old man opens his eyes. The shifting world opaque, heavy. Dark clouds swelling, turning. The old man blinks, pulls his head back. There's mud on the windows. Pliers on the floor. The world tilts away.

The old man opens his eyes. Vestigial movement drifts inside him. Recedes and reappears on the surface, bobbing. He finds his arm. Opens the door. The fresh air hits him.

He does not know how long he has laid there, minutes or hours. It could have been years and he is just now finding himself old. He grabs at the steering column, pulls himself up. The parts of him joined at odd angles and difficult to stack.

He stumbles down the lane. Eyes sore, swollen. He puts a hand along the stone wall as he staggers forward. Each swinging foot. The tractor and tank behind him, folded at the hitch. Filling the lane.

He coughs, head lolling. The breath tears at his throat as it rushes back in. His steps bundled in lurches, held tenuously together by the threads inside his legs. A hooded crow is perched on the opposite wall, shifting on its claws as the old man passes. Keeps a pale eye on him.

The old man hears humming. A tune. He stops suddenly, falls against the wall. Grabs at the stones behind him to keep himself upright. The melody rises, surrounds him.

Mary Flaherty comes down the lane, basket in hand.

The old man tries to straighten as she approaches, sliding back. The stones, wet glass in his palms. His breath loud. He watches her approach.

She wears a floral print blouse. Her greying hair curving over her ears like a tight-fitting cap, curling in on itself. She stands in front of him and stops humming. Hands folded to the side, over the basket handle. She leans close to him.

Íosac, are you well?

I am, he says. He looks down the road behind him, the tractor and tank out of view. Only empty, bending road.

You look worn awful, Íosac. Long day in the field?

The top ridge of the lane runs on into the valley. Into oblivion. He looks at her.

Mary Flaherty wipes the dust off his chest. Reaches up, touches his face. Wrinkled fingers on a weathered cheek, folding into each other. He flinches and settles. Wagtails dip and rise over the hedges, veer off and disappear. She steps back, looks him over. Íosac, a lady came asking after you. Real nice. Kind, I think. Is it alright I gave her your address?

The old man stares at her. Tilts his head.

You're a warrior, if nothing else, Íosac.

The old man pushes himself off the wall. Stands straight. He leans over to look in the basket.

Pears. Do you want one, Íosac?

Mary Flaherty hands him a pear.

The old man hobbles past her, holding the fruit. He stares down at it, turning it over in his hand. His wellies scuffing off the gravel.

THE HOLE IN THE GROUND

The old man and the child walk through the car park of the pitch. Holding hands. A slow rain filtering the daylight, the beaded drops in the grass shattered by their wellies. A wrap of wet ash on the ground, fading the colours of the earth.

The old man, the child, come upon the townspeople staring at the field. In the stands, along the fence. A few turn to glance at them, turn back. Their attention fully on the pitch before them.

As the child and the old man near they find the pitch without players. Instead, a few people slouch at the end. Hands in their pockets. The white chalk lines blurring into the grass, tattering. The old man takes the child across the field. A few of those on the bench following after.

What times we live in, what times, says the chipper owner.

They gather in a circle. Around a hole in the ground that they gaze into, that holds them there. The old man leans into it, blinks. Can't help but smile. The goal posts are missing.

Didn't really wake up today accounting for this, the trainer says.

They stare at the ground. Kick at the lip of the turf curled over.

That's some cheek, Jeffries says.

Lorry tracks lead away from the hole. Two lines swelling in the soft ground. A sulphurous haze rising from the wet pitch.

The Icelanders, I suppose, says the trainer. The trainer puts his hands on his hips and swings around. As if the posts might be in sight. Just overlooked.

Could be one of the teams from down south, Fox says. We nearly beat a few of them last year.

The chipper owner crosses himself. Fox sees it, does too.

We could say the rosary, the bakery assistant says.

The townspeople grab at their elbows and allow the rain to fall on their foreheads. Sometimes start to speak but don't. Rock on their heels from time to time. The pitch now a naked plane on which they stand vulnerable. Alone on the empty grass.

Eventually those on the field begin to settle back in the stands, join those already there. Sure, we'll drive around a bit, see if they dumped them somewhere, Hewitt says. But the rest slide to either end of the planks, making space for those sitting down. Bent forward, rubbing their thighs to warm them. They look into the grey shapeless sky from which the rain falls, to the cavernous ground, as if somewhere between them things can be explained. They do not go home, but sit there as they would the same time every weekend, silent, withdrawn. They watch the old man and the child cross the pitch, the car park. As if part of them, when it comes to it, suspects the child is at fault.

THE OLD MAN SPEAKS TO THE BULL

The old man carries milk to the heifers, cuts through the slatted shed. Holds the buckets away from him so as not to spill it on his trousers. Gates in the shadows rattle. The bull running his head along the bar.

The old man lowers the buckets to the concrete, exhales from the relief. Limps over to the bull. Rests his wellie on the lowest bar. The bull pulls back.

The old man leaves and comes back with a hessian sack of meal and reaches inside. Shakes the grain in the scoop before letting it fall to the bull's dish. Some of it bounces off the plastic and disappears into the straw around it. The bull snorts, takes a tentative step and then laps at the meal. The old man says, hell, and pours the rest of the bag into the dish. Some of it running over the bull's head and causing his ears to twitch. Have your day, the old man says.

The old man reaches to scratch at the bull's neck but the bull jerks away. Squares himself to the old man and lowers his head.

Settle yourself, the old man says, dropping his arms over the gate. Things are as they are. No reason to go mad over it.

THE NEIGHBOUR

The old man is on two knees before the discbine, the head's bonnet lifted up. His hurl among the spanners, ratchets and lubricant that mat the grass around him. The old man trying to loosen the nuts of the cutter bar and change the old blades. His hands wet with blood, WD-40. He stands up to exhale and wipe his forehead.

Colm the Pipe turns into the far end of the lane. Ambles. Talks to himself in a low voice.

The old man starts to go to the house but doesn't and then walks to the end of the driveway. Folds his arms. Waits for the plumber.

Colm the Pipe is fitted in his mass clothes. Keeps his head down and does not hurry. Runs his knuckles along the stone wall. Sometimes whistles. He stops in front of the old man. The top of his collar damp.

The two men stare at each other.

So, the Pipe says, and then says, well. He looks down the lane, starts nodding. Smirks. Then holds his hand out. I'm here to say thank you.

The old man starts to raise his hand and the plumber grabs it, shakes it. When he lets go the Pipe rubs his fingers together and then on his trousers. They leave a dark stain.

Can I see it? the Pipe says.

The old man follows the neighbour's gaze to the hurl laying

by the discbine. The old man shifts on his feet, squints into the daylight. Runs his teeth along his lips as he looks the Pipe over.

The old man picks up the hurl and gives it to him. The Pipe takes it in two hands and lifts it to his eyes, scanning the wood. She's mighty, he whispers.

Then he takes a step back and swings it left and right. Took the baptismal font, did you? he shouts. He turns around and swings again. Took the font, so? He flails the hurl and thrusts it around him. Lunges. Cuts it through the air back and forth. When he's done he lets the head fall to the ground and leans on the handle, catching his breath. Sweat skids off his jacket, falls to the grass. Finally hands the hurl back to the old man.

It was the font that got me the most, the Pipe says.

The old man takes the hurl back. Keeps it close to him.

But Íosac Mulgannon, the neighbour says. He grabs the old man's arm and squeezes it. The old man looks down at the Pipe's hand gripping him.

Well, says the Pipe.

The Pipe turns back the direction he came, walks down the lane. Jabbing his fists in front of him. Talking to himself.

MARY FLAHERTY'S VISIT

Mary Flaherty stands at the door of the house, basket of soda bread at her side. The milkers have just shut off, leaving an eerie silence echoing in the evening. She peeks her head around the corner, at the shed, sees only the bright and confused gaze of heifers looking back at her.

Ragweed grows along the edge of the house where the mower can't reach it, leans out like a fringe. No flowers or adornment. Just a worn path from the door to the cubicle shed. Mary Flaherty slips a bottle of holy water from her skirt and tosses it around the front door. It beads, glistens on the handle. She peers into the window, and then dabs the water on the end of her blouse and wipes at the glass to see more clearly. The cloth stained as it falls against her legs again.

Íosac trudges up the lawn, head bent low. His steps slow, drawn out. The child behind him. She waits by the corner of the house.

Being neighbourly, he says, looking at the bread, passing by.

Being neighbourly, she says.

He pushes the door and goes in, the child with the skull behind him. Leaves it open.

She sets the basket on the washing machine. Steps around his wellies, the back of them covered in manure. The shelves of the out-kitchen cluttered with fittings, calf boluses, ear tags.

Show ribbons nailed into the concrete of the wall, their ends curling and the blue colour fading to grey. Three dirty jumpers piled in the corner. The old man sits at the table, pulling off his trousers.

She turns her head. Eventually draws back a seat. Sits down gently.

Íosac.

The old man leaves the trousers bundled at his feet. Sits in his underwear. Dark purple veins flowing beneath his white bristle. He slumps, stares off.

The child sits on the back of the couch, his oversized socks on the cushions. The skull turned sideways. Motionless.

Mary Flaherty straightens her dress over her knees.

I'd offer you tea but I don't drink it, Íosac says.

I know, Íosac. How are you?

The old man twists his head further away.

A bucket sits under the table, half-filled with unopened envelopes, his name appearing again and again. Dishes on the counter, the range. One bread bag stuffed with other bread bags. The light over the table dim.

Íosac, are you alright? Some days you're here -

I'm here now.

No. I don't know that you are.

The old man leans back further, spreads his legs. The front of his knees quiver and still.

Íosac, do you need some help? With anything?

The old man grabs the edge of the table, jerks towards her. Did she send you? he asks.

No, Íosac.

There are no pictures on the wall, the wall blank and fading. Used syringes and penicillin bottles and other cattle medicine at the other end of the table. The sitting room unlit. The child, the skull, partly in shadow.

You're getting the same notions as the town, Mary, the old man says.

The town.

People get stuck on ideas.

There's people and there's ideas, Mary Flaherty says. You can't make an idea count for what is human.

Tell me of God then, Mary, the old man says, and walks away.

Before Mary Flaherty is an agricultural journal flattened from creasing, and half a cup of cold coffee. In the window she sees herself looking back, but behind it the rigid edges of the slatted shed, bleaching into the dark.

Mary Flaherty rises, takes the cup to the sink. Collects other dishes around the kitchen. Pans with grease in them, a pot with hard, naked pasta. Pours water over it all. She keeps her back to the sitting room. Stops. Fingers the cross in her pocket and turns.

The child still sits on top of the couch. The skull on its head, its fiendish eyeholes and wailing, mocking jaws gazing into some distorted future. The hellish stretch it came from. The wide boldness of the bone out of proportion to the small body below it.

Mary Flaherty approaches it. Her small steps resound loudly between the walls. Looks about her though there is no one else there. She hesitates, her fingers searching in her pockets for the crucifix again.

The skull turns towards her.

She hurries away, through the hall and towards sounds of rustling. Of water breaking and settling. She runs her hand along the wall, on its bareness. Feels its coldness cling onto the skin of her fingers. She pushes on a door half-opened and goes in.

The old man is in the bath tub. His paleness a shifting translucence under the water. He doesn't look up when she enters.

Mary Flaherty puts her hand to her forehead at first. Then lets it fall away in the stillness.

They say there's some things that are inevitable Mary, but I don't think so.

The old man takes a half-eaten packet of McVities off the rim of the tub. He holds them out to Mary Flaherty, but she waves them off. He thumbs a biscuit out of the package, slowly, and then takes a bite. Crumbs fall into the water.

You made your choice, Íosac. I won't pity it and I can't understand it. But what is it you want now?

He sets the McVities back down. As he leans back the top of the water stills and his thin, bent frame becomes apparent beneath it. Mary Flaherty realises that she did not hear the water running, that the bath must have been filled earlier in the day.

Is it just to die? she says. Are you arrogant enough to think that you'll be known for anything or even remembered for long?

The old man rubs at the skin on his chest where it was wet and now drying. Stood by it, he says. Stood by it sure. Now I just want it taken off me.

Mary Flaherty opens the press and reaches in until she can pull out a crumpled towel. She folds it over the hanger next to the tub. Shall I run the warm tap, Íosac?

The old man lifts his hand out of the water, turns it over in front of him, staring at it. Lets it slide back below the surface. Suddenly he turns to her, water splashing over the sides and spreading to her feet.

Don't tell anything to your sister about me.

Íosac, Mary Flaherty says, on the way to the door. She lingers in the frame. Peers into the darkness of the corridor, sighs. Finally turns back to him. That was years ago, Íosac. She's had a husband and kids. She doesn't think about you anymore.

The old man stares ahead. His knees sticking out of the tub like rusting angle irons. His shrunken chest slowly rising and falling.

She liked the way I played on the pitch, didn't she?

Yes, Íosac, Mary Flaherty says before closing the door behind her. The latch echoing in the hall. That she did.

THE PRIEST SPEAKS

The child rides in the bucket, his wellies dangling over the whitethorn, the gorse. The child lifted on the arms of the creaking machine, passes through the lane, held over the old man, the tractor bonnet. Draught cutting through the angles of the skull. The child above the turning landscape. Raised against the slate sky.

The old man steers with his hand in his lap. Shifts carefully, eases off the clutch without looking up. The shape of the road shakes the tractor, but the machine, the old man, is steady. The tread on the tyres leaves a fading seam on the wet road.

The vehicles that approach him still. The people inside look up to follow the child. The child drifting across the sallow glass of their windscreens.

The Ford crosses the bridge, enters the town. Does not hesitate at the traffic lights nor slow at the intersection. The townspeople on the footpath stop. The tractor's engine louder, bolder than the idling cars, the white line disappearing beneath it. The townspeople set their groceries on the concrete. Stand outside shops, lean in the door frames. The child was nearly taken from us, someone whispers.

The old man pulls back on the throttle, slows the machine before the Clarke Martin. Lowers the bucket before the pub's door, slowly. The child descends to the footpath. The hydraulic lines flinching inside their couplings. The child steps from the bucket, goes into the pub without looking back. Others follow him. The old man sits in the tractor seat for a moment. Runs his hand along the steering wheel. Then goes in too.

The priest leans against the wall, arms folded. Toothpick between his teeth. His eyes burn from the corner shadows. The echo of fluorescent light slides off the curves of his head. The folds of his soutane rippling over the polished wood as he breathes, straightens. He emerges from the back.

In the end times the dark horse rides, the priest says, walking into the centre of the room, head down. Black cloth sliding over his calves. The dark horse comes. We are told this.

Townspeople crowd the bar and the floor. Are silent. The seat next to Gill, Lonegan and Farrar is vacant. The child is on the knee of Lonegan. The old man grabs the back of the chair, glances up at those watching him, and finally sits.

Scale in hands, mounted high. Wheat for a penny and man's suffering for less. What one has, one will lose by word alone. It is so.

It is so, says Mary Flaherty, at the front table.

No man can hide from it. No man will be left unaffected, the priest says. His hook nose jolts around the room, turning on invisible trails in front of him. It will be dire, My Children. But My Children, man can choose how he stands up to it. He can choose who he is in the face of it.

The priest's shoes strike off the floor. Heads turn to follow him. The priest sways, and this pulls on his audience.

This man did, the priest says, pointing at the old man. This man stood against the tide of darkness coming.

Íosac Mulgannon, the Gardaí did not settle those boys from the east, but you did, Coonan says.

He did, says the priest. He looks around the pub, but not at the old man. Lifts his finger. Give Íosac his due, he says.

The old man holds the bottom of his pint on the table with a cupped hand. Stares into it. The veins of his arm cross each other like fallen electric lines. The heft of their eyes pushing into him. Because the priest is not moving, everything is still.

I was only looking after the child, the old man says.

He nods slowly. And then still nodding, pushes the hurl against the floor and raises himself up.

The child sits at the table, leaning forward on his elbows. The priest steps back to prevent from obstructing the crowd's view. The skull tilts and turns about the room, but there is no way to mistake the child's eyes inside it, peering from the shadows behind the bone. The townspeople tilt forward, inhale. The pub lights kept in the glaze on the table in front of him.

McGrane slams his hand on the table, stands abruptly. You can't take one of ours so easily, he says.

THE OLD MAN APPEALS TO THE CHILD

The old man turns on the lights of the shed. Small, muted explosions, veiled by cobwebs as the fluorescent bulbs flicker. Settle. The wrapped bales, the alley brush, the skid steer loader reluctantly emerge in the glow. The child is in the rafters at the end of the shed. The old man passes beneath him without looking up.

He flips on the vacuum, flips on the wash. Chlorinated water pushes through the pipes of the shed, shakes the braces that hold them. Cows in the cubicles do not stir. The hazy light falls on their backs and illuminates the dandruff on their loins and the stains on their hocks. They do not dully lift their heads to watch him change the gates, clean the water fountains. Do not flick their tails as he passes. They will rise when it is their time to stand and be milked.

The wash water empties into the dairy. A cascade from a higher pipe to the concrete, drifts to the shadows of the drain, joins a silent river below that pulls on the unseen parts of a man. Takes them away, soundless. The old man flips the toggle switch. Turns on the milkers.

Outside the dairy he looks up to the child. The child reaches for the cobwebs around him. Raises his hand to show how they wrap around his fingers. The old man stops, to say something, but doesn't.

He runs his hand along the first cow's flank to show her that he's there, and then dips her teats in iodine. His hands move automatically. Feels and does what they have always done. Works his way along the pit, wiping the udders of one row of cows before starting down the other. A familiarity to it that makes it neither absurd nor beautiful. The first milker on. Then the rest.

He stands there in the parlour. Coffee breath, the numbness of the cool darkness. The morning milking something apart from time. Among these first cows he does not think of what he must do for the day, weigh what he has done yesterday. Does not assemble the parts of his life. He does not allow himself to be sad, for himself, for the world. Nor happy. Because of that in this black early hour the holding area of the shed stretches before him endless.

Yet something tugs on him from outside himself. A feeling, nudging into him. A dark idea welling. He paces the pit while the cows milk, the claws clutching and releasing their udders. Something manky, he says, and when he says it out loud it becomes true. He goes to walk the alley but then decides that is a fruitless act and so takes a brush and sweeps it instead.

He pushes the stray silage against the bunks and when he gets to the end of the shed he puts the brush against the wall and walks into the dairy. Glances up to the child on the way in. Inside he stops. Looks around. Closes his eyes. The compressor is loud and fills the room. The violence of cooling milk. It fills his head. Pitchless roar that grabs at his bones. He opens his eyes and turns and looks and looks. Stares at the compressor. The control box. The vacuum pump, the pressure metre. The pressure metre reads the vacuum at sixty kilopascals. It should be fifty.

He bursts out of the dairy.

He throws his hands up at the child hanging above him, then turns to the cows milking to find the milk crashing inside the glass windows of the milking units, pulled too quickly. It is drawn with malignance from the animals, with greedy haste.

The inflations contracting with malice. The pipes in the shed resound the beat relentlessly, surrounding the old man, all the more malevolent because he now recognizes it. The cows shifting uncomfortably on their rear legs, swinging the milkers between their hocks. The shed throbbing with adrenaline.

It's not the way it's supposed to be, the old man says.

He pushes back into the dairy, the door recoiling on its hinges. Stands in front of the vacuum metre. Hits it, as if it is the thing itself and not a thing that only measures. Through the inlet pipes the sound of milk hurtling into the top of the bulk tank, shattering the pool inside. He hits the stick again. Paces over the weathered concrete. Looks up to the child as he shoves through the door.

What would you have me do?

The door snaps back on the spring and bounces against the wall, causing the cows closest to it to stir. He descends into the pit, leans underneath a cow to take the milker off. She lashes her switch across his face and he grabs her tail, the whole of its bone in his hand. Turns the stopper and pulls the unit off her. Her teats pink, rings of puckered flesh at the top. The inflations of the unit fall over his hand like a wilted flower. He turns the valve again and it heaves excitedly.

God damn it all, he says. The heavy gasp of the shed around him. Pushing in. He runs up the steps. Picks up a pitchfork and hurls it into the alley. It bounces end over end. He lunges into the dairy again to kick the vacuum pump. Reads the metre again. Stomps his foot—wash water rising around him, bursting on the concrete. Out the door again.

He stands below the child. Are you going to help me now?

The old man holds up his arms for a moment and then allows them to collide against his waist. His eyes clammy under the fluorescent bulbs. His skin a crude wrap over his bent frame. I don't understand why it's like this. Child, speak now. Child!

The child does not look down. He sits slumped on the

rafter, head cocked back. The skull open-mouthed, half-grinning. Stares at the bottom of the tin roof.

The old man storms into the parlour and knocks everything off the pipe. Paper towels lift apart and fall damply to the aisle. The iodine jug rolls and spills, the dark liquid pouring over the stone ground on its way to the drain, turning brown and then yellow as it thins.

The old man lowers to his knees below the child, looks up. The child kicks his heels off the beam. The bottom of his wellies float above the old man like vertigo spots. Take it, the old man says. He lays on the ground, curls himself up. Take it all, he says, his words drowned by the pulsation of the shed.

Take it all.

THE ICELANDERS

The old man, the child, walk the lane in the dark. The old man lumbering between the stone walls. The child follows behind him, dragging his feet. Night-birds flutter between branches. Lift into flight as tittering shadows. Sometimes the old man speaks to the child. Tonight he does not. To speak to the child is to tell of things he does not know until he says them out loud. To come upon things he does not want to know. Sometimes he does. Tonight, instead, he walks the lane.

Sometimes when the old man walks at night he likes the idea of how everyone else is sleeping but he is awake. Conscious. It makes him feel he has one-upped the world for a moment, outlasted it. Outworked it. He lifts his hurl and runs it across the brush. Shattered leaves trail behind him. The darkness, it is his, he allows himself to think.

The old man does not know songs or verse, but if he did, he ponders, this might be the time to recite them. He knows only the sounds of the land, of the farm, and the rhythms he puts to them and them to him. He has stories, some his father gave to him and those he came across himself. The time the east field was called the Lime Pile Field because of the supplies the county kept there. When he unhooked a wagon and it rolled through the hedge all the way to Mary Flaherty's. All the wet spots and backward calves and times the cattle got out. Sometimes he tells them to the child, even if he has told him already. As the child is the last to keep them, so must he keep the child.

A humming noise creeps along the wall. Channelled by the stone. A course melody, cadenced by spitting. As they near it the old man grabs the child, keeps him close. Puts his hand over the mouth of the jaw and then realising the child does not speak, pulls him behind him. Hurl poised.

There is a figure on the wall, feet spread. Tall, lanky. The shape of a teenager, his features concealed in the dark. He faces away, sways. Pisses into the hedge.

The old man reaches up his hurl and pokes him.

The boy jolts. He flails his arms, urine dropping over the rocks. Christ fuck almighty, the teen says.

Joe Hyland's garage is up ahead, the door open. Sounds of stirring inside. The old man grabs the child and walks below the silhouette fumbling with his trouser clasps.

Where you going auld one? The teen tries to follow on the wall, straight-legged. Attempts to zip and walk at the same time.

The old man steps into the light of the shed. Puts the hurl over his shoulder. Inside two boys carry an air compressor across the concrete floor. They see the old man, freeze. Look at each other. One jerks his head towards the open door of Joe Hyland's trailer.

You're hardly Hyland, the old man says.

A nephew, says one of the boys. Grey hair, moustache, but young. The other one is shorter, shaved head, tattoos. As the eyes of the old man settle the shapes of four more boys emerge from the back shadows, their arms full of tools and appliances. Watching him.

The old man looks toward the house at the end of the lane. The house is dark.

The boy from the wall rushes in, panting. Under the garage bulb he is a tall, awkward ginger. Snuck up on me, he says in a Dublin accent. The auld lad's a fucking ninja.

The grey-haired teen and bald-headed boy pick up a PTO shaft, but the grey-haired teen drops it when he sees the child. The plastic shield shatters. The teen peers around the old man, to the child. Reaches up to touch the skull. That's some dark shit, he whispers. He motions to the other boys to come closer but they remain in place, looking at the old man, the door.

By fuck, you're the Icelanders, the old man says.

The old man sits down on a tractor tyre. The hurl between his legs. Then the old man laughs hysterically and it echoes between the tin walls, washes over them. In the flesh and blood, he says.

The grey-haired teen grabs a pipe wrench and holds it over the old man. You better mind yourself.

I couldn't care less what you do, Lads.

He's playing, the ginger says.

Is he playing? asks the grey-haired teen. The grey-haired teen laughs himself. A high-pitched cackle like a crow.

Two boys pull spanners off the wall in bunches, hold them like kindling in their arms. Others start to tentatively lift plough parts and a workhorse towards the trailer.

The Icelanders? The grey-haired teen puts his hands on his hips. Looks to one side. Then the other. Fucking A, I like it Sham.

They start to lift an old radiator. Decide it's too heavy. They scan through the garage, tossing aside couplings, fittings, an oil filter.

You did the church job? the old man asks.

God is good, Sham, says the grey-haired teenager.

The bald-headed kid says, especially when you sell him to the city churches.

The ginger puts his palm over his heart. My grandfather looked over a small country parish. They shut it down, see. He had these things in storage when he passed, bless him. Must have kept them, sure.

The old man claps his hands together. Rocks backwards.

He nearly collides into the child. And the instruments?

The ginger pretends to play the banjo.

Christ Almighty, the goal posts?

For the craic, like! the grey-haired teen shouts. Slaps his knee and howls. He allows himself to collapse onto a bucket, his limbs settling around him. Red-faced, teary-eyed. Turns to the old man.

You're not too torn up, Auld One? Us grabbing the goods?

Unto Caesar what is Caesar's.

Amen, shouts the ginger. This shitehawk town. Sure, we started hanging about during the day, for the hell of it now. Sure, who's to bother?

The grey-haired teen bites his lip, studies the old man, his hurl. These people, they must have done you hard. He sticks his foot out to half-heartedly trip the bald-headed boy carrying an anvil. The bald-headed boy steps over his runner. That, or you're a real hard cunt.

The ginger holds up pliers. For work, Boy! Sticks out his tongue at the old man. Tosses them in the trailer.

The grey-haired teenager stares at the child. Seems to be making calculations. It's hardly our fault, he says. Quiet, serious tone. It's the way the world went. Beyond our control and all that. He starts laughing again. What's the deal with the kid?

I suppose the world made him that way too, the old man says.

The other boys walk around the old tractor, bare workbench, a rusting wall fan. Their hands behind their backs, stooped. Turning things over to consider their value. Picked the bitch clean, the ginger says. Let's roll.

The grey-haired teen rises. Starts towards the lorry cab, then turns back to the old man. I'll tell ya, we'd fucking bash ya in if you tried anything, you know yourself.

The old man lifts himself off the tyre. His knees cracking. Sure, what are you going to do to me that hasn't been done already? He looks himself over, shrugs with a half-smile.

By Jays, the state of you. You're right! We'll take the kid.

You will not, the old man says.

The grey-haired teen grabs the child. The old man pulls the child away from him.

The bald-headed boy opens a switchblade knife. Metal sliding against metal. It rings inside the garage.

Listen Auld One, we'll do no harm. Just need a little insurance, the grey-haired teen says.

We have a Gardaí scanner, the ginger says. Motions towards the lorry.

The grey-haired teen shoves the child towards the other two. The child winces. The skull looks up to them. As long as we don't hear nothing on it about no thieves or nothing we'll drop him off at the next town. He can take the bus in the morning. The teen snorts. We'll give him a few cans while he waits.

It is only when they clutch the sleeve of the child that the old man realizes that he has seen them before. He grips the hurl with both hands.

If you're sound he's safe, sure, says the bald-headed boy. Shifting on his feet, chewing gum.

They pull the child towards the cab. The child turns back, reaches for the old man.

You will not take the child, the old man shouts.

The Dublin boys lift the child into the seats of the lorry. Telling each other to be quick. The child sits with his hands in his lap. The ginger lifts his finger to touch the skull, but another boy elbows him first. The trailer rocks from the weight of the teenagers inside it. The back door slams shut.

The old man runs into the road. Stands, throbbing. Both hands on the hurl. A hunched shadow in the lane.

The headlights flick on. The old man awash in a yellow glow.

See, he's buckled, the grey-haired teen says. He tugs on the seatbelt over the child's chest. Safe and sound. The words come muffled through the glass.

The child is pinned between the older boys. Small, ill-fitted. The skull looks out, expressionless. The ginger waves the old man out of the way.

The grey-haired teen puts the vehicle into gear. It creeps ahead. Jesus, man, clear out. The teen shifts again, the lorry bouncing. Picks up speed.

The old man spreads his legs. Braces. The exhaust of the lorry is blue in the night and trails after it. The stones in the wall blur by its doors. Tools spill against themselves in the back, followed by cursing. The grey-haired teen bangs the heel of his palm on the top of the steering wheel. Looks to the child. The ginger leans his torso out the passenger side window and waves his arms frantically.

The old man's eyes shine wild in the headlights. He raises his hurl above his head and clenches his teeth. Heaves it at the windscreen of the lorry.

The old man falls to the ground from the momentum swinging through his body. He looks up in time to see the blade of wood entering the glass, dissolving it. It lands over the boys inside. The truck sways left, right, screeches. It crashes into the rugged wall. Stones collapse around the tyres.

The old man hurries to the passenger door. He allows the ginger to drop out of it. The youth lays mumbling on the road. Blood on his lips. The old man unfastens the seat belt, pulls the child towards him. Glass sheds off his clothes and bounces in the lane. He bends down and picks up the hurl.

The grey-haired teen and the bald-headed boy are sprawled over the bonnet, twitching, moaning. One lifts his hand towards the old man, but the old man is already lurching down the road, arm around the child, disappearing into the darkness.

THE OLD MAN MILKS

The old man stands before the storage shed. The night heavy around it. The shed where the farm empties its trouser pockets and heaps the things it sloughs from it in case there's something to be called into use again. His resistance, stacked upon itself and pooled into shadow. Without the flicker of the rafter bulbs his body's memory leads him around the corners and rough edges of duct fans and broken rake shafts, the shapes of bolts and nails under his wellies pressing into the rubber as he passes over them. He reaches into the darkness, finds the handle of the generator, thrusts it forward.

The old man flips the toggle. The cowshed lifts apart into light, the flaring glare shocking the stone and walls and animals inside it. Wash water erupts through the pipelines, pulsing through the building. The cows raising themselves in the cubicles, backing out slowly. The motor of the generator booms, but slips into the folds of the throbbing between the walls, spreading into the night.

He milks. Takes the iodine dipper off the pipe, dips their teats, wipes them. He strips each teat, feels it in his fingers, remembers to put balm on it later if it needs it. He sees his arms and his hands move in front of him, and he too is a thing bleached by the overhung bulbs of the pit. He guides the inflation over the teat, gently. Sometimes the child insists to do it and he lets the child. In those times he stands back and watches the child and the cow.

The old man milks twice a day. All of his adult life and most of his childhood. Same time every morning, every night. His mind and body diverge. The body knows what it will do, probably knows the mind is not to be trusted anyhow. Often the old man has gathered the cows from the pasture and set the milkers to wash and dipped the first udders before he realizes he has done so. If he were to die tonight, the old man knows, his corpse will rise the next morning and set the milkers to wash.

The shed windows frame a peering face. The dust blurring it, the whitewash chipping on the wood around it. The head drops back into shadow. It drifts in and out of the panes as it slips along the outside of the shed.

After passing the last window the builder stands in the doorway of the parlour. Waiting to be seen, invited into the fluorescent carry of the pit lights. Finally lowers his head and steps in.

The old man bends towards a cow. A milker in his hand.

The builder runs his palm along the animal's thigh. Nods.

The old man nods.

The builder looks at the cement walls, the cobwebs in the rafters. Avoids the eyes of the old man as he scans the rows of cows, his lips mouthing the numbers in their ear tags.

The old man takes the inflations off the front teats, leaves the back ones working. They heave, pulled tight and dangling.

I do the big sites, you know, the builder says. Sure, pays the bills.

The old man grabs the parlour hose with his free hand. Sprays the manure off the cow's hooves. He tilts the milker to flush more milk. Do you like it?

The builder taps the pit wall with his boot. Been meaning to stop in, in the way of things, he says. Even asked the priest about it. He said you don't bite or nothing. A small smile appears on the builder's face. Then he says, probably.

The old man takes the milker off. Hangs it on the clip. Dips another udder in iodine. His movements among the cows rigid, deliberate. He fumbles taking the paper towels from his back pockets. It has been many years since he has milked with another man in the parlour with him. He keeps his head lowered as he wipes the teats, strips them.

The builder turns around him, takes in the shed again and the things inside it. My auld lad did some farming. Part of me wishes I kept it up. He stops suddenly. Sees the child in the rafters, in the far corner of the building. The skull turned broadside, gazing at an empty wall. The thin legs of the child dangling beneath it. Cast against the rafters the skull holds nothing in it but shadow. The builder looks away, then looks back.

The Casey place, was it? the old man says.

It was.

I remember.

The builder puts his fingers in the iodine. Brings it to his nose. I guess I'm trying to take account of things, he says. As anyone should.

O'Flynn comes through the door, sees the two of them. Looks down and blushes. The steps bend beneath the bulk of his wide chest, thick legs. He has a plastic bag in his hand, the top rolled in his fist. The shapes of cans bulge on the bottom.

O'Flynn kicks at the rubber mat beneath his shoes, bites his lip. Turns between the two men. Finally opens his bag and sorts through it. Gives one can to the builder, one to the old man. Wanted to drink with the lad who stood up to the boys from the east, he says. I'm not much with words otherwise.

The old man keeps his can by his waist, holds it gingerly. O'Flynn opens his. It snaps, foam rising. He exchanges it with the one the old man grips.

So.

They touch cans.

The old man breathes in. Beer, shit and iodine turn inside his chest.

A shadow flickers outside the window, draws the old man's gaze. The darkness inside the panes settles. The old man watches, nearly goes up the steps. With his arms folded he swings his head to look over the milkers, sees that the milk still flows.

Were you scared? O'Flynn asks. I would be.

I guess I just don't know if I was wrong about you or not, the builder says. If one thing changes that or what it means.

In the silence they watch the old man. The cows stir in the pit, bumping into the railing. The milkers swinging. The men avoid each other's eyes. Their heads nod, barely perceptible, to the rhythm of the vacuum's pulsation.

The old man climbs the steps of the pit. Hurries toward the shed door, open and tilted on its hinges. Limps into the night air that moves through it. The old man steps outside, at the edge of the fading light bleeding from the cowshed, and stares into the fields.

The old man stands before the dark plane that spreads beyond his farm. There were the lights of the town and the lampposts that held them and the dust-to-dawn bulbs along the roads. Now after the blackout there is only emptiness. He knows where they are, but it is only his memory that puts them there.

He stares out, and the more he stares he sees the darkness ripple before him. His eyes settle, survey the billows of rolling shadow that move across the land. They pass through hedgerows and rye and the stand of alders, drawing towards him. Silhouettes pulled by the beating pulse of the shed. They emerge, narrow to shape. Take the form of Heffernan, Rogers. Ó Maoildhia. Trudge through the grass and sometimes look up to the open shed door.

They've come to say thank you, the builder says, standing next to him now. I don't know about sorry, but they'll say thank you.

The old man turns and leans against the wall. Thinks he feels the shed move against him.

The people come to stand around the old man, surround him. The smell of silage bales and grain dust drifting between them. Goldenrod swaying along the edge of the shed. They shift on their feet, wait for him to speak first. The pulsation of the milkers push behind the old man, spread through the door, the concrete. They beat in time, repeating what he has known them to always say: the child, the child, the child, the child.

CONVERSATION WITH FARRAR

Farming, farming, Farrar says. Mulgannon why ask?

They stand in a knot of trees, in the darkness, the trees an island among the dark rise of ryegrass. The cans they hold limp at their beltlines catch a bit of light, the men themselves but shadows. The night thick with stars, the stars overlapping and twisting over each other.

Farrar stands with his free hand tucked in his collar, elbow hanging over his chest. I was then I wasn't, he says, and then says, farmer.

The old man drinks. The trees are thin and branchless, bending over the men. The tops of grass rustle and then are still. The field a murkiness that swirls around them.

Neighbour says, says do you want to raise some heifers for me. Farrar swings the beer can in a stiff arc. Nope. I was a farmer but now I'm not. That's the way of it.

The old man leans against a tree. Rests his weight on his hands behind him. Lets the rough bark scrape at his skin. The leaves folding below the moon as it drifts over. Sometimes I want to feel like I deserve it, the old man says. The way things have gone. I would nearly do bad farming.

The child, Farrar says, throwing up his arms. The child.

I had farming and now I have the child, the old man says.

Farrar sighs, the shape of him folding. I was angry ... always. Don't know why. But I know why.

The trees shift over them, creaking. Dew forming on the uncut hay, lifting up the smell of the ground. The silhouettes of bats pulse over a distant hedgerow, the flicker of their wings only heard when the wind is still. They rise out of the horizon and merge into it again, cross over each other.

Cúchulainn knew that it was phantoms calling him out and that he couldn't win, but he fought anyway, the old man says. What do you think of that?

Farrar turns suddenly and puts his arms around the old man. The stubble on his cheek scrapes against the old man's neck, the half-empty beer can pressed into his back. Holds him as the moon reflects off the moisture on their wellies.

Farrar lets go. Turns back to the field and heaves his can into the darkness. Angry, angry, he says to himself, walking into the night.

THE PRIEST SPINS THE OLD MAN

The shed lights glow from the rafters and wash the concrete below in filmy ruddiness. The pulse of the milkers fill the building, bleed quietly into the night. The old man leans on the manure scraper, half uneaten biscuit in his mouth. His wellies next to a dark shape on the pocked concrete. He pushes the grizzle from his teeth, spits into the grates. Watches the priest enter the parlour.

The priest pulls up his frock and stuffs the ends of it into his jeans. It bulges around his waist. When he leans over the pit wall to take the udder of a cow in his hand the cloth looks effeminate on his large frame. The priest kneads the cow's rear quarters in his fingers, sends a flush of milk through the inflations. When he decides she is done he turns the stopper that kills the vacuum and lets the unit collapse over his knuckles. Strips each teat between his fingers, slowly, deliberately, shattering streams of milk over the concrete. It pools and is blue under the shed lights.

Ever had sex? the old man asks.

Have you ever ate margarine?

The priest rises and walks along the row of cattle to find the cows the old man has not yet milked. He places his hand on the Friesian's flank to steady her, leans forward again. In the early days of seminary they loaned us out to farmers. A way of serving the needs of the congregation, I suppose. I only ever wanted to save the town.

The cow rocks on her hind legs again, the milker swinging below her. Don't, the priest says. He holds the inflations in place. Were you baptized? he asks the old man.

In a water trough. It's still in the pasture.

The clergy would do that?

If that's what the old lad would let them. He had humour.

The priest looks up, cups his chin in his free hand. Is your soul saved then?

Just made trouble for it.

The cow thrusts her hoof and strikes the priest in the wrist. The priest recoils. Pulls his fist back and hits the cow as hard as he can. The cow jolts and swings away from him. The milker drops to the grates. Sucks in dry shed air. The priest tilts his head and grips the lip of the pit, a deep release rushing over him.

The child sits in the rafters of the shed, on top of the stack of wrapped silage bales that fill the back of the building. Feral cats coil around him. He lets the heel of his wellies bounce off the white plastic as he watches the things below.

The priest rises. Sits on the wash bucket in the middle of the pit. Were the cows drinking from the water you were baptized in?

They were. And they drank from it afterwards. It was their trough.

The priest reaches underneath his frock. Pulls out a balled-up Dunnes bag with tobacco and papers. He stoops over the bucket, filling two cigarettes on his knees.

Has this been our lot from the beginning? the old man asks. Predestined, in your terms.

I want to hate, says the priest. But I'm only allowed to hate faceless things. Things that don't know I'm hating them and wouldn't care.

The old man sprays at a pile of manure in the grates, watches it lift apart. Spits again. When I was a boy, on this place, my older brother used to put me on his shoulders and spin me around as fast as he could. Don't know why I started thinking about that again.

The open windows along the wall like portals to the darkness outside. The shed light pushing against them. The milker units on both sides of the pit throb, steadily, each rhythm its own and discordant. Broken stalls, an empty feed cart and bale wrapping shoved against the cracked walls. Chaff scattered along the feed bunks.

The priest turns to the old man and bends on one knee. Keeps his hands lifted, as if to catch the farmer.

The old man stares at him and then looks at the cattle around them. Takes a step forward. Leans. Doesn't know how to put himself onto the priest.

The priest waits.

Finally, the old man tips forward and falls into the other man. The priest lifts the small crooked frame of the farmer to the air, his wellies hanging in front of the priest's chest, the priest folding his arm over the back of his legs. He turns slowly, the priest a pinnacle beneath him. The features of the shed, the cubicles, the cows, the drinking fountain, where he has spent his waking life, shift around him. Each bucket of meal and tangle of wire turn and disappear and circle again, surging faster and blazing into light as the priest spins. The old man is lighter the faster he turns, lifting into the air, towards the ceiling. The old man rises, higher, higher, until not the priest's hands nor the rafters nor the shed can keep him anymore.

When the priest sets the old man down the old man lifts his foot and is flung back. He stumbles until he collides against the pit wall, sends the bucket skidding. Finally slumps to the ground in a heap. In the sudden stillness of the shed there is only the distant pulsation of the milkers beating around him. The priest grabs the front of the old man's shirt with both hands and brings him to his feet.

They stand in the open doorway of the shed, looking out

at the sweep of darkness over the valley. The priest hands the old man one of the cigarettes, lights it for him. They blow the smoke into the night, pale apparitions drifting in front of them. The old man spits.

God help us if these were things we've chosen, the priest says. The two men hold their cigarettes at their sides. Embers pulled into flame before burning away.

THE TOWN GOES DARK

The old man drives through the skirts of light beneath each lamppost. Leans back, arms folded. The steering wheel wedged between his thighs. Mind, body, machine welded by the unconscious while he drives and that's why he drives, now, through the town at night and it is so he can think. He moved bales off a south field but instead of turning into the shed he kept straight, driving on. Until he found himself passing along the main street of the town in low gear, turning around at the butcher shop, and going up it again. Passing beneath the lamplight.

Town is an invention born of fear, he thinks. First man came and then man farmed, and then those who couldn't farm drew together and put their houses close to one another so as to not have the space to be of anything themselves. He drives. The tractor tilts as it passes over drainage grates. The streets are wet and spread the lamplight unevenly. The shopfronts on either side of him like a wilting hedgerow. Gaps of shops already abandoned.

The old man knows that it is coming. It is a whisper behind him. A fingernail drawn across the back of the neck. A bad feeling that is natural with farming, but things are coming and the things that are coming are greater than before.

He thought he is here to clear his mind, let the grizzle settle out of his thoughts. To tell himself he will yet stand, and if that is true then perhaps he is here to call out the thing that approaches. To present himself beneath this municipal light and declare that he is here, he is here, he is here. Still.

Shadows pass by the windows of houses. Curtains close. The old man drives on.

He stops outside the butcher shop. Instead of pulling in and turning around again he leans in the seat. Scrapes a clump of mud off the window and lets it fall to the floor.

The streets go dark. The lamplights, the shop signs all dampen out. Everything to silhouette. The town extinguished in one industrial glitch. The traffic lights dull like dried fruit in the late autumn. He can still make out the corners of buildings on the street, the metal posts that hold the traffic signs, their lettering gone. He wonders if he has done this with his mind but he knows he has not. It is the belly of the dark thing passing over them. It is coming for them all.

He puts the tractor into gear and drives home.

THE OLD MAN OPENS A LETTER

The old man swings two buckets at his side, walking from the house. Collides them together to make the plastic echo when they meet. So sometimes I'm here and sometimes I'm not, he says. Swings the buckets over his head. Fast enough that the envelopes inside don't fall out.

He walks into the shed, not waiting for his eyes to adjust. Shoves the buckets below a cow's chest as she stands in a cubicle. Leaves them there as he tries to squeeze in beside her. She reaches back to sniff at them, lifting the corners of those on top.

The old man dumps out the unopened letters. They flitter and settle beneath the animal, covering the sawdust of the cubicle. The logos of feed companies, debt collectors, solicitors pile over each other.

The cow shifts her weight, flicks her tail. She lifts her foot and sets it down and lifts it again, unsure of what's beneath her. Pressing her hoofprints over the envelopes. The wet manure absorbing into the paper, curling it.

Some cows, seeing the buckets, walk along the bunks towards the old man, their heads bobbing. They stretch their necks over the brisket bar, bawl. Rub their heads against a post if they stand next to one, course hair and dandruff flaking to the concrete.

The old man tosses the buckets in the alley. One lifts

upright, the other rolls to the grates. He's about to push past the cow again, but stops, reaches for an envelope. Wipes the bank's insignia on the front of his jeans and then opens it.

He sits for a long time, gazing past the print. To the pitchfork against the wall. A broken shed fan. A tipped bag of milk replacer.

THE FIGHT FOR THE CHILD

A patch of grass between the house, the shed, and the heifer pens, tangling over itself. The old man stands in the middle of it. The head of the hurl on the ground but he does not lean on it nor slump. The child behind him. The farm looms over the child, dimming in the twilight. A cow pushes into the gate of the cubicle shed, the chain that holds it stretched taut. She lifts her head and bellows into the dusk.

The door of the grey saloon claps shut. An erect silhouette strides along the grass. Shoulders above the fading horizon.

The old man puts both hands on the knob of the hurl. Waits for the banker to come to him.

Calm day, O'Grady says. He stops before the old man with a packet of documents at his side.

The old man has seen this day in the darkness of the morning while he drank his coffee and every time he stood in the alley of the shed with his arms folded, watching the cows milk out, every time he has laid down at night. The bad feeling that puddled in his gut for so long it went into his tissue and ligaments and stained his thoughts now wells out to stand before him. To see if it can swallow him. He had hoped for a heart attack, in the shed. Extinguished in one go. Or to be taken by an accident, sometimes fantasising the pain. That did not happen, but he will not mourn for that now. He wonders if he can meet this with grace, but he knows that he cannot. He is a man called to stand.

You will not, he says. Then says, take my farm.

Paul O'Grady, a man with acquired professional demeanour. Stares at the ground and rubs the ends of his vest between his fingers. Íosac, look.

The old man sticks the end of the hurl in O'Grady's chest and pushes him back.

O'Grady's face goes blank. He blinks.

Íosac. The skin on O'Grady's forehead reddens. He opens his arms, the envelope in one hand. I need you to sign them. It'll be easier.

The old man looks up. The sky is stone, this he knows, and maybe man only stands to be crushed beneath it, but let it crush him. Let it do its worst and see if he asks for mercy.

I need to put these in your hands, O'Grady says. Acknowledge receipt of the papers. This is the way it is supposed to be.

The old man swings, knocks the packet out of his grasp. The envelope lays broadside, leaning in the grass.

You're mad. You're fucking mad.

Heifers stand before the fence, watching. They are wide-eyed, poised to dash at any moment. The birds of daylight have settled inside hedgerows and tucked their heads into themselves, leaving the air empty and swelling. The old man is rigid. The smell of iodine rises from his clothes, pools behind his eyes. The child stands behind him, blowing from inside the skull. A distant rush of wind from inside the bone. The skull tilting, as if on its own, towards O'Grady.

O'Grady rocks on his feet, clicks a pen at his side. His features receding into the dark.

Another car pulls along the road, stops at the edge of the driveway. A woman leans out of the open door of the vehicle a long time, and then rises. Becomes a looming profile from the other direction, between the house and shed. A bounding shadow striking towards them.

The old plough, the teat dip drums, the broken radiator are a silent theatre.

She marches into the soft grass, a ground that holds the curve of the old man's wellies every time he passes over it. It now reshapes around her steps. Scribes them, as if the ground can tell a story and keep it. The woman straight-back, clean-faced, greying hair short. A tree that does not bend in the wind.

Íosac Mulgannon then. She looks coolly to the child. To the old man. You're hard to get in touch with, she says.

The old man reaches back, feels the child.

The woman's grey eyes trace him. Narrow. I'm from the Department of Children and Youth Affairs, Mr. Mulgannon. I've sent requests to meet with you personally, but without that pleasure I've had to conduct my own research.

She, too, has paperwork she presses against her chest.

The grass between them bends. A slick thin sheer, meandering the ground. O'Grady stoops over it. Picks it up.

Slow worm, he says. It curls below his hand, tilting towards him. Tongue flickering like an electric current. He holds it higher. Didn't think you could find them around here.

Its mouth silent, bared. It jerks, twists erratically. Half of it drops to the ground and slithers away. O'Grady still holds the tail, a brown chord twitching in his fingers. Are you taking the child from him? O'Grady asks.

I am, the woman says.

O'Grady throws the tail in the grass. It writhes, coils violently before them.

The woman steps on it with her shoe, and then slides the shoe along the ground. Stretching a grey film before her. It was my charge to assess you, Mr. Mulgannon.

The old man strikes her on the head.

She recoils, stumbling backwards. Her body folds and she falls to the grass. The documents leap before her. She puts her hands over her ears, gasping.

Child, listen to me now, he says. We are the Mulgannons. We stand on what is ours. Let it tear itself from our feet before men take it from us. We do not move. We do not yield. O'Grady paces back and forth, his fingers spread over his face, whispering oh, and when he changes direction he starts to curse and then stops and says, oh, oh. He takes a step towards the old man and then throws up his arms and starts pacing again.

It's the milking and the feeding and the fieldwork, the old man knows. The throb of the milkers, in the pipes. In the shed. And the milk falling to the tank. The scrape of the fork against the bunks and the long draw of water a cow takes in gulps. His feet colliding against the inside of his wellies. The wild swing of a calf's tail when it's on the teat. And the ache of it all, of all of it. It's the rhythms of these things that fill him, the move of it in his bones, that drown himself inside his skin. He has worn himself into everything here. How is it that he must give up that which is his? That which is the all of him.

Behind them a black shape shifts along the field, its dark relief against the murky horizon. Tilting side to side, stalking. It grows to be Young John Allen. His steps artificially large in the tall hay, his knees lifted high. The top of his hat gives a broad shape to his head. He nears, the rye scraping against his trousers.

Christ Almighty Íosac, he yells as he comes upon the woman. He bends low and offers his hand.

She slaps it away. Tries to rock onto her knees. And then stands, red-faced. Brushing her cheeks with an open palm. I'm reporting you, she says, pointing at the old man.

O'Grady turns from them. His wrist on his forehead.

The eyes of the old man are bright. Pulled by any movement. His chest heaves. The child stands behind the old man as the woman collects her papers, pulls at her collar. The child looks to the three visitors. The bone sliding over his pale skin. His arms and legs shrouded in the tattered jeans, stained geansai. He looks to the old man. Measuring, the old man thinks.

Young John Allen stands between the old man, the woman. Half-turned. Seems I'm a bit late, he says. No one turns to him or appears to be listening. O'Grady paces. The custody agent furtively blots at the corners of her eyes. Young John stands with his hands on his hips, looking over the sheds, the house.

Young John Allen walks to the heifer pens. The heifers dart back at his approach, but then take a timid step and stretch forward. He puts a work shoe on the lower rung, drops his head. The heifers sniff at his hands and he lets them. They tug on his shirt with bloated eyes. Lick at the skin on his arms with their rough tongues. Finally, he pushes himself off the gate and returns to the others.

I'm here to say my piece, so I'll say it. Íosac, I think the boy should come live with me and Molly. We can do good by him. We can do better for him. Look, he'll still be on a farm and we'll look after him well.

The ground flickers. Slow worms curl over the earth, plaiting the grass. Raising their heads. One slithers over the wellie of the child, its smooth skin against the rubber.

Jesus, O'Grady says. He kicks one away. Íosac, will you take this envelope and let me leave?

The old man does not speak. Does not stir. He holds the child in his grasp and the skull is more vivid than anything else around them. The sky darkens. The old man and the child's silhouettes fuse into the skull, a beastly body joined to its bone. The ground throbs at their feet.

The five of them wait in silence as the farm turns to leviathans around them.

It's the pulse of the milkers, he once believed, and he believes it still. It gets inside you and pushes you and pushes you and carries you. It takes the place of your heart and it hollows out your veins and fills you until it is the only thing inside. It's not the changing of the season nor the time passing. It's the beat of the inflation that you hear even after you leave the shed or settle in the kitchen that pulls you out of yourself and away from other people and marks you as different. As a farmer and nothing else, and the old man could be nothing else.

Two stoats steal past the corner of the heifer shed. They stop at the edge of the grass and rise up, narrow faces that scan what lays before them. They jolt. Stare at the child. One slinks ahead, belly in the grass. Then the other. They watch the child, poised to lash.

One of the stoats bites into the grass, paws it. Clenches a slow worm and then shakes it out of its teeth. The animal's thin tail lifted as it makes a shuddering cry.

We need to get the child away from him, the woman says. For his own good.

The old man flinches at the mention of the child. Tilts his head.

The old man's hurl is raised and catches a faint luminescence from the dusk-to-dawn light on the front of the shed.

The custody officer comes forward. She starts to extend her arm towards the child, but the old man steps in her way.

Young John Allen takes his hat off, runs his head through his hair. Looks back towards his own farm, as if he can see it beyond the fields and hedges before him. O'Grady takes his pen from his vest pocket, clicks it a few times, and puts it back in. Wrings the envelope in his hand, over and over. Finally puts it in the back of his trousers where it flexes, reshapes.

The custody officer reaches for the child again but the old man jerks the hurl towards her and she flinches, jolts back.

The plate cooler in the dairy kicks on, echoes in the farmyard. The shadows of the three visitors draw closer to each other, bunch. Their breath pale in the night. The quiet rustle of the grass around them as the slow worms push through it.

Suddenly O'Grady thrusts forward and grabs the child's arm.

The old man clutches the other hand of the child but O'Grady pulls harder, and when he wrenches him out of the old man's grasp O'Grady and the child are flung backwards.

The crack of bone splits the dark.

There is silence among the silhouettes in the grass. They stand between the shed and the house, still, nothing but bulges in the night. O'Grady lifts himself, gingerly. No one helps him. Instead they look to the old man. The shape of him, his hurl. Still holding out an empty hand.

The child cries. Huddled on the ground, folded. The shattered skull lies around the child's bare head, the shards bright and sharp in the blackness around them. The child's own face small, pale.

They gather around him, unsure. They want to offer their hand. To touch him, lift him up, but they don't. His geansai is cut, torn. Tears on his cheeks, without light to reflect them as they drift. He looks up at them, mouth open, throbbing. He searches them, reaching his thin arms out. The old man stands among the other three, leaning over the child. Reaches down and touches his face for the first time since he slipped the skull over it. This is the only time he has seen the child cry.

God help us all, Young John says.

ARRIVAL

The stretch of his legs, body, half-lit in the haze of the dusk-to-dawn light. The rest shadowed by the wet concrete walls. Wellies slid off his feet. The old man leans back on the overturned bucket, his eyes closed. The plate cooler of the bulk tank turns on. Then shuts off.

The old man pulls his legs in and is about to rise but doesn't and sits straight-backed. Teat dip barrels next to him. On them stripped nuts and bolts and washers like an old currency. The mart slip of a heifer he didn't want to sell. The sink drips. The old man rises to take the letter and plane ticket tacked behind an old breeding calendar. The moisture around the floor drain shimmers. He sits, unfolds the letter on his lap, stained and ink-dulled, presses the ticket to his chest. Bends the top of the ticket as if about to crush it but stops before it creases. Whitewash chipped off the wall floats towards the drain. The old man says a woman's name in the dark.

The words of the letter turn in his head, in his voice and then hers. Telling him it was too late Íosac to come over. She had waited and then moved on. The plate cooler kicks in. He stands abruptly and scatters the wash water in the channelled wear of the concrete and goes to an open farming journal on a teat dip drum. Turns it a few more pages. The dour headlines bleeding into the shadows. The old man sits.

Leaning back, bent like a fork tine. His breath echoes. The

smell of teat dip fills him the more he inhales. Tightens his throat. He slides the unused ticket along his stomach, down. Pins it to the front of his trousers. Rubs. Wash water ripples below his wellies. The plate cooler turns off. He rises and unbuckles and leans over the teat dip barrel. Sets the ticket on top and closes his eyes, forehead against the wall. His knuckles rapping against the barrel's hard plastic. The dusk-to-dawn bulb flickers in the wind, spreading jarring purple light.

He stills, exhales loudly. Wipes the wet slick of his hand on the open farming journal. Crumples the pages in his fist and sits. The old man leans back. Closes his eyes. Opens his fingers and lets the pages fall to the concrete. Wash water climbing their edges.

The old man against the cold wall and he is not sure if sleep finds him in dreamless hollowness or if it is the quiet night passing. Several times he draws his wellies beneath him and thinks he should go to the house but doesn't. He listens to the sink drip until he thinks they are words and then doesn't listen. The skin on his cheeks and forehead clammy in the moisture of the dairy and he notices again the smell of the teat dip but doesn't know if it is from his clothes or the barrel next to him. He thinks again of going to the house but doesn't and doesn't know why.

Something stirs in the silence. He might have felt it before he heard it. It lifts him off the bucket, through the door.

The shed lights are bright that he stumbles under, the stiffness and tiredness of his limbs causing him to lurch. The noise he is drawn to is jolting. Is the call and rankle of birds. A figure lurks in the blackness at the end of the shed.

A boy stands framed in the doorway, holding his mineral gaze upon the old man. Thin and slight, his skin the colour of grain dust. His eyes the worn metal parts of old machines. He reaches towards the old man.

Jackdaws crowd behind the boy, shrieking. They feign at him and then hop back, huddle into each other. Yellow eyes darting in manic angles. The old man stumbles forward to scatter them. They lift up, but collect around the boy again.

The old man starts to walk down the alley and then comes back again, wellies scraping against the concrete and bunching chaff in front of him. The boy still reaches for him and the old man sees the boy has been bitten, the pale flesh of his arm punctured by canine teeth. There is no pain on the boy's face, and the old man looks into the night and sees nothing. A brown rat bursts from the chaff, at the boy, wide-eyed and berserk. The old man steps on it, turns his weight into it. The crunch of bone muted inside the fur. It pulses under his wellie. The old man lifts off his foot and the rat drags itself, broken. Heaving towards the boy. The old man kicks it into the darkness.

The old man places his hand gingerly on the boy's shaved scalp. Scans the shadows around them. Whose child are you? he says. Steps forward into the boy's outstretched arms. Embraces him and lifts him off the concrete. Whose child are you?

ReADING

Trousers and undershirts spread across the floor, still half wet with manure stains. Blue paper towels cast among them where they had fallen out of the back pockets. The sloughed skin of milking, of the ghosts in his bedroom. The curtains drawn. The old man tucked in the corner, knees to his chest. The child is not there.

And Cúchulainn seized his weapon on account of this advice, both for his honour and for his valour, although he should come to the end of his life. And beautiful, sweet music was sung for him by noble and illustrious artists, and there were women carousing and playing board games, and there was mirth and merriment around him on all sides.

The old man suddenly rises and sits on the edge of the bed, bunches the duvet behind him. He twists the book's binding. It does not give, tear. He scrapes at its covers with his fingernails. Throws it against the wall. Opens the dresser, pitches the book in, slams it shut. In the silence he listens for things stirring outside the window, but there is nothing. He stands in the unlit room, a silhouette with his arms across his chest, head down. His clothes spread across the floor like his distorted reflection. He reaches for the knob of the dresser.

The old man kicks at the trousers, pushes them away from him. Settles in the corner again. Opens the book.

THE
STORM

Malachy freezes, places the glass and the rag on the counter in front of him. He stares at the stained cloth bending over the rim, as if connected to the words from the radio. Malachy waves his arm, trying to silence the few patrons there, prostrate anyway, as he turns up the volume. The deejay's voice drifts over the empty stools and tables in shadow. The men inside rise to their feet, slowly. Stand in front of the window. They stare at the grey, blank horizon to the east. Seemingly empty. Seemingly far away.

Cars pull off to the shoulder on the road that leads out of town. People stand in front of their open doors, looking into the sky, the same voice throbbing from the dashboards. Others walk out of their houses but do not notice their neighbours doing the same, because they all stare at the same hill line that marks the highest field, and the unknown and coming push that exists beyond it. The mechanic sets down his power drill and the butcher lets his apron crumple on the floor. The clerks at the SuperValu no longer scan groceries, but sit slumped and dazed on their stools. Little by little the town falls silent. Stills.

The radio delivers the report without flourish. Describes it as an unstable air mass, the size of which has not been experienced for two hundred years. Descendent of Oíche na Gaoithe Móire. The Night of the Big Wind come again.

It could carry destructive forces unseen by any generation living. Could culminate into wind shears to destroy everything in front of them. It might pass entirely over the island. If it does touch land, there is no way of telling where. The announcer tries to keep his report measured, but at the edge of his words is a fear that slips away from him. His voice echoing through the shops, the houses in town. The town knows it will not pass over.

The next morning people go to work. They pull up the blinds and take their messages. Check their stock. But as the day continues many businesses grow quiet and vacant, phones ringing unanswered. Most of the shop doors are left open with the lights still on. In case anyone still has need for something inside. If something is taken from the shelf usually a bill is pinned under a stapler or paperweight on the counter, but never collected. The cafe and pubs where people run into each other have only empty chairs tucked against tables, the tables pushed against walls. The people in the streets scattered, their pockets bulging with batteries and matches. Their heads tilted towards the east where the storm is said to come, to the sky that hangs above them, thinking that they can already feel the wind turning somewhere faraway. The playground at the school, usually full of the clatter of flailing children, falls quiet. Only two or three pupils sit cross-legged, gazing into the distance. A rubber ball strayed into the hedge.

The boiler attendant puts a garden chair under the bridge and sits in it. He tells people he doesn't know if it's brilliant or daft, but when the world comes crashing down this is where it will find him. Some climb onto their roofs to check for loose tiles, shaking each slate in turn, as if their hands were a mock storm. Their spouse and children loiter below them, arms over their chests. Some families collect their grandparents, if they're living alone. Others try to find a relative or friend without trees next to their house, if they can, bundling their duvets into the backseats of their cars. Some stop at the church to light a candle. A few slip it into their pocket instead, in case they'll need it later. The choir sings hymns in front of the doors all day, members rotating in and out to take refreshment in the hall. How Great Thou Art. Nearer My God to Thee. They sing their favourite ones first and then work through the hymnal. Their voices drift eerily through the muted and empty town, falling into the background of people's thoughts, going unnoticed.

Malachy nods to the old man and the child, rises off the stool to pull him a pint. Gill, Farrar and Lonegan sit out of reach of the grey daylight. Empty stools around tables, some turned upside down. Most of the glasses packed in crates, against the wall. Some planks nailed in front of the windows. Other boards lean next to them.

Kiera Malone, Gill says. Sits back, arms folded. She was the best ride I've ever had.

Lonegan pulls the child onto his lap, bounces him on his knee. The child's limbs thin, loosely colliding against his sides. The child looks to the old man as he is jostled.

It was one of the summers I worked in the butcher's, Gill says. The counter was sort of rough cut lumber. It left dimples in her arse cheeks.

I could take the child and go somewhere else, but you know I won't, the old man says.

Farrar waves off the idea. Leans half-turned from them, scowling. Tucks his hand back in his collar.

The men sit quietly, bent over their glasses. The pints warming before them. Not unlike the silence passed among them through the years in the same corner, same shadows of the pub. Stains on the table where it has weathered beneath their hands.

Something tidy about being taken in one go, Lonegan says.

Farrar sharply turns to him, his arms in the air. You don't know that we're so fucked!

Sure, look it, says Gill. We're old bastards, either way. Might as well shake hands while we're able for it.

Lonegan runs his palm through the child's hair, letting it slip through his fingers. The child's head looks small, naked. His skin paler in the shuttered light. As if a thin shelter for the things inside him.

Ye can go, the old man says. Cut out of town and take your chances.

The worse shag I ever had came from this fat bird with a cold, Gill says. It was like she was snarling while I was putting it into her. It was Farrar's sister.

Farrar turns to him. You did not.

I did.

She was wide alright, Farrar says. Shakes his head. God alive.

Gill takes a long pull from his glass and then tips it towards the old man. We're here. We made a choice. That makes us better than most.

Then Gill stands up. Grabs the top of his chair and flings it against the wall. It rattles across the floor and skids to a stop, a leg rolling, twisting, until it disappears under a stool. He tries to lift his foot high enough to get on top of the table. The other men rise, grab his elbow, shirt. Help him up.

Now, he says, turning around, his shoes knocking over the stout. Glasses breaking as they fall. It was one hell of a pleasure, ye sons of bitches. He reaches down and takes the old man's hand and shakes it. The table wobbling beneath him. Gill's smile settling, fading as he looks over his shoulder to the window.

Not a single leaf bent by a breeze in the days before it comes. The hedgerows do not stir, nor does the hay in the fields shift. The small stands of alders parcelled along the valley are rigid and stoic, the whole landscape fossilized in place. The ground, usually bothered by the Atlantic mist, stiffens beneath the grass. It is thought that a little wind or a small cloud burst would be the storm tipping its hand, or its strength leaking out before it. The stillness unsettles everyone.

Many houses burn turf during the waking hours of the day, for the comfort of the smell. However, they do not stay in their hazy sitting rooms, but stand in their back gardens, watching the fumes curl into the sky. To see if they can, perhaps, tell how high the empty firmament runs above them, or maybe make an offering to it. Smoke rises from the chimneys in the town like twisting ladders, those watching it half expecting it to become part of the swelling thing that will crash down upon them.

The old man returns home, moves the calves from the hutches to the alleyway of the cubicle shed. He carries them in his arms while he can. They blatt and squirm against his chest, shit on his trousers. When he tires he sets them down and leans against their weight as they lean against him. He pulls them ahead in bunches. Later, he walks the windows of the shed with boards over his shoulder and a mouthful of screws, the metallic taste moving down the back of his throat. Scans the weeds along the shed, the bunks, for old parts or tools that might still have a use, but leaves most things as they lay. He stacks round bales outside the rear door and then nails it shut. Thinks about doing the same to the front, but then figures someone will have to get to the cattle eventually.

The old man is washing the bulk tank when Young John Allen calls into him. Young John pulls his tractor behind the shed, a shining titan among the scattered ruins of old tyres, teat dip barrels, a rusting hay rake. His eyes red and tired as he slouches across the lawn, wellies scuffing.

I suppose it's still hay-drying weather, he says. Gives a nervous laugh.

The old man stands in the doorway of the dairy. Finally steps aside and holds the door.

If one thing doesn't get you, the other will, Young John says, ducking beneath the old man's arm. That's farming.

That's farming, the old man says.

The child sits on the overturned bucket in the corner,

watching a piece of chaff float towards the drain and fall over the edge. Young John conscious not to look at him.

I actually consulted with my engineer, he says. The fellow that helped me design the place. You know what he said, about the wind and such? Go into the silage pit.

The old man rinses out two cups laying in the sink basin and rubs out the stains with his fingers. Water splashes on his shirt. He grabs a jar of instant coffee off the control box, taps some granules into the cups.

Is that not a daft sounding thing? Young John Allen says. The pit is big enough and the silage around it will hold the walls in place. We're parking all our machinery in the opening to keep the debris out. Engineer said they're big enough that next to each other they won't tip over.

The old man holds each mug under a stream of hot water from the tap and hands one to Young John. The dark liquid foams, crackles. He lifts up a half-filled cup of milk replacer. Young John waves it off. The old man shakes some into his mug and then places it next to the instant coffee.

Come join us, Íosac. Both of you.

Thanks a million.

Young John Allen stomps his foot, scatters water across the lower parts of the wall. Grabs his hat rim with both hands and bends it. Why won't you mind yourself?

Going to stand by what's mine.

That doesn't make sense.

Doesn't have to.

Young John Allen takes a sip, turns towards the door. Places the cup on top of the teat dip barrel. I don't think I'm a bad man for doing what has to be done.

The old man puts his hand on his shoulder, shuts the door behind him.

The day before it comes a hush falls over the valley. It is a deeper quiet, one that magnifies the silence that has already descended on the town. It is only in the late morning that the first person realizes there aren't any birds. The air absent of the call of crows and no rooks crossing the horizon to the tops of other trees or to pick at the plastic on the silage bales. Those that have known the wagtails cutting above their heads and scurrying into the brush when they walked the lanes have them no longer, and without them they are left with a shared loneliness.

On the eve of the storm there is nothing left for the old man to do but milk and feed, and to take the day as he has taken all the others. When he moves among the cattle he does not linger to rub their ears or caress their necks. They have no use for pity in the same way that they cannot give it to him. He removes the top layer of silage bales to open the ones on the bottom, the best second cutting he has left. The cattle turn their jaws heavily, sometimes fling the baleage in front of them with a jerk of their heads. In the afternoon the old man fills a five gallon bucket with water and alley lime. It has been years since he has whitewashed the walls. They have darkened and stained in the dim shed light. Because he does not have a paint brush he wraps his geansai around the tines of the pitchfork and dips it into the bucket, pushing the liquid over the concrete. The sleeves knot around the shaft as if arms clinging to it. His hands move up and down the walls, back and forth, pulling away the wear. The shed with a deep stone smell. The old man carries the bucket to the other side of the building and runs the forkhead along the end of that wall. The top of his wellies turn pale from the dripping cloth. His jeans become stiffer with the lime drying in the fabric and it feels good to keep the same motions against its resistance. Cats race up and down the aisle, their tails in the air. The air grows brighter as the inside of the shed lightens and is lifted from the shadows. When he is done he dumps the leftover whitewash through the manure grates and passes through its blinding whiteness, out the door.

When night falls the old man milks. He moves between the

corroding dividers stretching on both sides of the pit, bent and dislodged from their braces. The milkers throb around him. The child crosses into the shed by the side door. Walks along the feed bunks, among the heads of cows. They strain towards him with their mouths gaping, hot breath rolling out. Their tongues lapping at him. He places his small fingers on the hard bone of their foreheads, which makes them only more frenzied to take a piece of his clothing in their mouths.

When the last cow has been milked the old man hangs the claws in the dairy and sets the system to wash. Chlorinated water floods through the inflations and crashes against the inside of the plastic windows. He pushes the baleage back in front of the cows that have nudged it out of reach, collapsing the halos of forage in front of their muzzles. Gives each one their normal scoop of meal, the grain clattering heavily against the tiles. He is about to close the top to the bin when he decides to fill the cart again and gives each of them another scoop. They lift their heads as they shatter the pellets in the back of their teeth. When he finishes he turns off the lights of the shed without stopping to turn around and look. In the dairy he shuts off the wash cycle and a deep exhaling sound fills the room as the vacuum pressure escapes into the night. Ending the pulsation that rang into the valley.

When it comes the people of the town can hear it long before it can be seen. It starts as a feeling. As the unease among the people in a room or the nagging thought that cannot be swallowed away. It is a whisper everyone thinks they heard but cannot be sure of. Each person looks to someone else expectedly, but does not receive a response. It draws into a light droning, so thin and indistinct at first that it is difficult to place and seems to be growing from within the people themselves. Then the noise billows and rises, raising in pitch as if it is climbing the horizon, just out of view. Some people can't help but to look out their windows before family members pull them towards safer places. The force of it expands and swells. Embodied in a darkness reaching from the east like a stain broadening over the sky. The rush of wind and rain tears at the things at the furthest edge of their sight and as it comes towards them the sounds it brings grow more menacing and industrious as it means to tumble over them.

It sweeps over the plain and the grass is pulled tight and turns pale, so both the sky and the ground hold a spreading border of the nearing storm, the storm pressed between them. Sleet and then hail shatters off the stone fences and collides into itself, building up in the crevices and brush around it. Hedges are stripped and raked, half-torn and mangled, scattered about the headlands. Boreens and lanes and jennet pastures are assaulted under driving rain and ice that knifes the ground. The loosest stones of old sheds and cottages topple and pile at the base. Sometimes dragged away in the wind.

Branches crash against the post office, the building on the farthest edge of the town. Its sign pulled upside down on its chains and then flung upwards into the sky. Whirls end over end as it climbs out of sight. The gutters are torn off the side of the bank and skid along the sidewalk. The screen of the ATM chipped and flaking.

The slate sky, empty for so long, now turns heavy with the swirling debris pulled from the town. Tiles and rubbish bins, traffic signs, lawn clutter thrash into each other above the streets. The wind mauls houses where they have stood for decades crashing onto their roofs. The more the storm rages the darker the air grows with the shards of the town intent to extinguish the daylight. The gates of the mart swing furiously from their posts and the front of the SuperValu collapses. The doors of the church rattle and then swing open. The stained glass shatters onto the pews, the priest sitting behind the pulpit.

The old man stands in the shed, faces the child. He lifts his scarred hand and touches the child's cheek. The child's skin is smooth and pristine, and the old man believes that he has never himself been so untarnished. He realizes that even though he is old and bruised and marked it does not matter because the child is beautiful. He thinks that he has not kept the child, but that the child and he have kept each other. Then the old man laughs. He laughs loud and although the growing wind pulls at his voice it still echoes through the rafters. The child stares into the old man's eyes and the old man believes that the child has found him worthy.

The old man had taken a suit from the tailor's shop when it had been abandoned and put a new cigar and lighter in the front pocket. But the suit remains folded on his bed, and instead he pulls the cigar out of the back of the jeans he milked in and sticks it in his mouth, chewing the ends to grit. He had kept the cows in the cubicle shed and they bawl at the gate and push against it. He leads the child into the dairy and lifts him up the steps of the bulk tank. The steel walls still wet and a dampness swells through the opening as the old man lowers the child inside. His small feet make a hollow echo when he lands. The old man places a ladder in there. The child seems to understand that the old man is not getting in there too because he does not reach for him or beckon him inside. The old man tussles the hair on the top of the child's head and walks away.

The old man enters the cubicle shed. He taps his hurl against the stalls as he passes, rust flaking below them. The sound reflecting off the walls. He spits the cigar grizzle onto the concrete floor. Walks out the end of the shed.

The hailstones sting his face, ricochet off his smile. They stick in the folds of his clothes and matt the hair stretched over his head. He steps forward, the end of his shirt rippling wildly behind him. The front of his wellies pushing into the wind as the wind itself tries to resist him. Thrust him back. A teat dip barrel spins as it skids across the ground. He stands before his open fields, the grass bent flat and slick at his feet. Clutches the hurl with two hands. Confronts the sky.

Bale plastic, calf buckets, spare milker parts hurtle around him. The door of the machinery shed is gone and the plough in the front shakes violently, the shares rattling against the cement. Hydraulic lines and tyres are flung across the driveway, blur into the wind. Pitched rubble collides against the old man's body but he does not move. Feels the pull on him grow and so bends his knees, lowers himself. Grips the hurl tighter.

The roof of the cubicle shed clatters, bangs against itself but he does not look behind him. He's pushed back a few steps, catches himself. Plants his feet and lowers his shoulders further into the wind. Stands. Every bit of strength in him put to meeting the storm. The ice, the debris pelt his face and distort his vision until he cannot see in front of him, but he doesn't look away.

The wind batters him and drives into him and plunges at his chest until it finds a way to enter him. It flogs his mind and pulls him from his memories and from what he is. Tears at his skin. Means to crack him and shatter him asunder. To lift him and wrest him from his place on earth and discharge him into nothingness and leave him with only this final resounding act. He tenses, braces. Stands.

Until there is nothing left to stand against.

As the wind settles the insulation of houses falls quietly over the valley. It lands soundlessly in the wet grass and catches in the scoured branches of the hedges that still remain. The drift filters out the light of a dull sun that hangs above the town. The glass of the traffic lights is cracked and casts its thin colours over the blanketed litter. Flower stems lay flat over the lip of the footpath, their blossoms pulled away and their leaves tattered. Some buildings stretch half-spilled into the streets, their roofs mangled and hewn. The stop sign carries scratches from the debris pulled across it. The lamp posts stand as stripped pillars, one of them bent from a falling tree. The river that weaves around the town is the only motion on the landscape, and its push against the rocks the only sound heard.

Morrissey rushes out of his home and leaves the door open. Instead of examining the battered houses or damaged shops he keeps running. He stops at a car without windows and looks into it just to be sure. His steps resound loudly as the debris crunches under his shoes, tilting him to and fro. He calls out for anyone that might need his help, stops to listen for a response, and then runs again. He climbs a pile of shattered concrete and stumbles. Picks himself up and keeps going.

Cosgrove and O'Mahony stand at the end of the street, picking through the wreckage. When Morrissey pushes past them they follow him out of town too. They cross the bridge, looking wildly around them. The nearest fields are the most heavy with the town's flotsam. The stone walls bear large gaps and lay heaped in some places. The hay is pressed flat to the ground, showing the contours of the rocks beneath it. They run until they cross into the last of the wind brushing against the damp stones. It pushes into the men, pasting their shirts against their chests, lifting their hair until it finally dissolves into silence.

The old man stands with his hurl in his hands, head lowered. The joints and shafts of machinery, equipment, half-buried in the grass around him. His geansai torn and gaping over his back. The skin that shows is pale, bleached. His ear bleeds and the blood falls to the ground.

The three men watch him and he does not move. His legs spread, tensed. Shoulders bent. His eyes cast down.

His chest heaves, faintly.

CLEARING

The blade scrapes along the driveway, slowly, a thin dust lifted up as the metal grinds over the stones beneath it. The shattered boards and branches, sheared tyres and a ripped tarp bunch, swell and turn together, then trail off the side of the bucket. The Ford creeps along, slowly, steadily. Pushing away the debris in front of it. Leaving only small pieces of plastic or snapped twigs in the path it makes.

The tractor crawls past the heifer shed, its windows shattered and the side of the building scoured and cracked. The storage shed with its roof half-torn away and hanging. The cubicle shed, a pile of boards stacked in front of it where the old man pulled them away to start the morning milking.

The child sits on the armrest of the Ford, erect and rigid. Stares at the old man as the old man stares ahead. Keeps the tractor straight.

The wreckage of the storm heaps before the tractor and falls away. Folds into itself on both sides of it. A teat dip barrel rolls in front of the machine, catches an old tyre, lifts up and tilts away.

The lonely droning of the bucket abrading the earth spreads over the debris around it, fills the cab of the tractor. The old man does not turn on the radio or sing to drown it out. Instead lets it surround him. Take up the space inside him. The child staring at him. When he reaches the end of the driveway he turns into the lane, runs the bucket along it.

The stone walls that pass by the side window are ragged. Cleaved and tumbled and sometimes scattered into the boreen. They roll and grind in front of the tractor, eventually push together and resist the machine. When this happens the old man lifts the bucket, angles the Ford, and dumps them into the hedge.

The old man turns the Ford into the first field. Comes to rest on the headlands. Pulls the parking brake and stands on the top step.

The ploughed ground before him lays heavy with the ruins of the valley. Like a strange and feral vegetation, the surface of the land lifted and laid atop itself. Spread between the gangly hedgerows, leaf-torn and in some places bare to the stones that have been pushed into them through the years. A wooden crate, roof slates of the nearest houses. The rusting bumper of an old lorry. A part of an aluminium roof bent awkwardly over the field.

The old man ducks his head back into the cab. This was to be my end, he says, lifting his hand to the clutter laying jagged over the furrows. He slaps the child's shoulder and shakes his head and says, but even that storm couldn't take me.

The old man stands on the top step of the Ford with his hands on his hips, looking out.

The old man stares and stares, does not move. Does not speak. Runs his tongue over his lips but that is it. Gradually his shoulders soften, bend. He stares and does not blink and does not seem to be looking at anything. Exhales.

The old man descends the steps, grabs the end of the aluminium. Starts pulling it towards the hedgerow.

THE OLD MAN VACCINATES

The old man opens the gates of the crush, herds the heifers towards it. Throws up his arms and shouts Heya! and pushes into them. They sniff at the opening, lower their heads and push back. When the first one lunges through the rest follow, kicking their legs in the air and colliding into each other.

The old man slides the bar of the headshoot back and then steps through it. Picks up a bottle and syringe out of the chaff and holds them both in his palm, works the plunger with the other hand. Flicks at the syringe and presses the air out of the needle. Drops it by the side of the shoot.

The heifers bunch, push into each other at the far end of the crush. Lift their heads and stare back at him wide-eyed. He throws himself between two animals, their withers at his chest. Cleaves a black heifer away. She tries to turn into him but he thrusts ahead with his waist. Presses her towards the shoot and when she's close puts his shoulder into her thighs, forces her in. Reaches over and closes the bar.

The old man feels her neck with two fingers, pierces the flesh with the needle. Empties the plunger. The heifer jerks and then stills. He lets her go and she scurries back, squeezes into the rest of the animals huddled in the corner.

The old man refills the syringe. Drops it in the chaff. Puts his arms over the top of the gate and lets his head sink and stays that way. Finally climbs back in the crush.

The old man tries to pry a heifer away from the wall but they shift and scatter, knock him against the gate. A heifer jogs by and the old man steadies himself and kicks her in the ribs. Grabs another heifer by the neck and pulls her towards the headshoot.

The old man is filling the syringe when the shopkeeper pulls open the door and looks in. A small bundle tucked in one arm. He sees the old man, nods, and hobbles to the front of the crush. Rolls the bottle over on the ground with one of his shoes to read the label. Puts his foot on the lower rung of the gate and scans the pen.

The old man opens the shoot and climbs back in with the heifers.

You didn't pick up your bread, bacon and McVities, the shopkeeper says. He thrusts the bundle at the old man as if desperate to get rid of it. Today I thought, ah Jays, he didn't pick up his bread, bacon and McVities.

The old man puts his arms up and tries to block a heifer from getting around him. She lowers her head, closes her eyes. Pushes herself through his grasp.

The shopkeeper takes the groceries out of the sack he brought. Holds them over the top bar of the gate.

The old man puts his hands on his hips. Watches the heifers circle the crush. Finally takes the groceries from the shopkeeper. Tosses them into a five-gallon bucket in the corner of the alley. Turns back to the heifers.

The shopkeeper stares after the old man. The clerk's face is pale, flushed. His mouth doesn't come to a close at rest.

The old man weaves himself among the heifers. One that was already vaccinated stands in front of him and he pushes her out of his way. She jolts ahead. The old man grabs the base of another heifer's tail and steers her towards the shoot.

It all just keeps going, doesn't it? the shopkeeper says.

The old man fills the syringe, stabs the heifer behind the shoulder, lets her go. Climbs back into the crush.

Well, the shopkeeper says. Slaps the top bar. Crumples the sack in one hand and walks out the door.

When all the heifers have received their shots the old man opens the gate to their pen and steps back. A few eye him, toss their heads, but as the others rush back to what they know, they too, do the same. He shouts at the last one and she jolts through. He closes the latch after her.

The old man grabs the syringe, bottle. Wipes the glass to check the level inside before stuffing it in his back pocket, pulling his trousers tight. Kicks at the chaff and finds an old syringe and picks it up as well. The dust rising around his legs.

He stops at the five-gallon bucket. Leans over it. Instead of reaching inside he turns off the shed lights. Closes the door behind him.

CRUSHED

The old man ploughs.

The child with him, in the corner, the old man having set down a bundle of sacks for the child to sit on but the child has bunched them against the glass. His reflection in the window filtered by the dust in the air.

The soil cast before the mouldboards, turning over the calm. The ground soft, tilting under the tyres. The radio plays, but in its static falls indistinguishable from the sounds of a working machine. The shares rise up intermittently when hitting rocks, then slink back into the ground.

The child sits with his legs to his chest. Leans on his knees. His body rocking to the shape of the land. Sometimes the old man thinks of things he would say to the child but he does not say them. He thinks the child prefers it this way, but perhaps only because he himself prefers it. The child is with him and he still has him and that means things. That is something they both know and does not have to be said.

He looks behind him to find ground unturned, a strip of weeds swaying. A share stuck upon the coulter and hovering over the field. He puts the tractor in neutral and lowers the throttle. Has one hand on the grab bar but looks at the child a long time. The child stares ahead. The old man pushes through the door, descends the steps.

The old man looks up to the sky out of old habit but

knows that it holds nothing for him. He follows the greyness and expects it to be bunched at the edges or rimmed in shadow. Lighter towards the top where it might thin. But it is undifferentiated. Steel. Is a grey that passes through the trees and the space between leaves, stills them in the daylight. Presses on the horizon.

The old man kicks at the coulter, the share. He takes a large stone and throws it against them. The sharp edge of the disk already cutting into the mouldboard, wearing a groove. The old man lowers himself to the ground at the front of the plough so he can kick at the share at a better angle, kicks at it.

The tractor lurches ahead. The plough collapses on the old man.

The tractor itself rocks to a stop but the sprung pressure of the mouldboard slams into the old man's chest. The air leaves his body in a carnal gasp. Rushes into the sky. He stares up and sees nothing. His ribs flexed on the verge of shatter. His arm flails, strikes at the ground. The pulse of the engine transmits through the machine and overwhelms his own heartbeat. He pushes his head back, strains. Feels the iron grip him harder. Sees the child in the back window. Framed. Everything around him in shadow. The child watching him.

The old man waits to be taken up, to be borne by something larger. To be dissolved into nothing but the memories of what he did, what he stood for. He is ready to be of the things that make the land. To be part of the story that it tells.

The lever, the old man tries to say. Lift the lever. Only a trickle of air comes out. His mouth shapes the words, trembling.

The old man swings his arm, feels it brush a small stone.

He strains, pushes against the ground again to see the child. The child doesn't move.

The old man's vision blinds into glare. His breath becomes short, uneven. It is harder to push his chest against the world around him. His own self has pooled in the scars on his body and this ploughshare now collects it all beneath it as it presses him out of his thoughts. His body and mind parting. He knows now that he was loved by the child.

The old man scrapes at the earth around him, in short, disjointed stabs. His eyes bulging, unmoving, as he wheezes. He gives in to the euphoria of finding himself overwhelmed. The swell of relief as the parts of himself still on the earth are stunned away, gathered and piled in oblivion.

The child descends the steps of the tractor. Its engine heaving faintly. The exhaust from the smoke stack disappearing above it. The dust of the field has dulled its paint, decals. Its couplings rusting over the hydraulic lines. Its bucket bent, dented. The machine now seems small and empty. Fading away in the daylight.

The child approaches the old man beneath the plough. He does not bend down closer or reach to touch the old man. Does not try to feel the last warmth of his skin. Only stands by the farmer, leaning over him like a shelter that is too narrow.

And then the child walks away.

The child crosses the open field, his wellies pushing into the heaved soil. He steps over shattered rocks, half-buried weeds. Around a tangle of fencing wire that had blown onto the land and had been turned by the plough. He does not examine the broken plastic and shed tools and old bolts that sometimes stick up from the ground. His footprints following after him, fading. It is not apparent where he is going, because nothing lies before him but the empty horizon.

He trudges through the cluttered ground, his back to the old man, the distance between them becoming greater.

THE OLD MAN LETS GO

The old man, the child, sit in the rafters atop the shed. The whitewashed walls, the cluttered alley stretch on. The cows crowd against each other below them, throwing their heads into the hay. The old man straddle-legged, head bent down. The old man had unwrapped all the bales, shoved them to the cows. To have them fed when the wind comes upon them. The tops of their backs like a heaved landscape shifting beneath the ceiling.

I used to climb up here and jump into the baleage when I was little, the old man says, speaking to his wellies. I'm surprised I remembered that.

The child stares ahead. Rigid-backed, balanced. As if built into the shed itself.

The old man straightens. Puts a hand on the top beam for support. When it is done do as you must. I know that you will.

The plate cooler in the bulk tank kicks on. Makes a muffled drone behind the alley walls. A feral cat trots the length of the building, weaving in and out of the empty cubicles.

The old man looks up from the cows. I have stood against it all and to the end, haven't I?

227

The old man takes a package of McVities out of his back pocket. Bites a biscuit in half, tosses the rest of it to the grates below. It falls into the wet manure.

The old man grabs the front of the child's shirt in his fist. Don't forget that you were a Mulgannon.

The child stares ahead. Leans only as far as the old man has pulled him towards himself.

The old man lets go. It doesn't mean much to those out there, he says. The child's shirt remains bunched, crinkled over his small chest. Collar drawn down.

It meant to me.

Below the sound of hay sliding against itself as the cattle pull it from the bales. Dust rising above them like a veil in the dim shed light. They lift their heads and toss the forage over their backs, onto the floor behind them.

The old man stares at the child a long time. One cow bawls and then another raises its head and calls out too, their necks heaving and briskets swinging in front of them. They bury their muzzles into the baleage again.

The old man lets go of the higher beam. Leans back, slowly. He feels the momentum take over and unhinge him from the rafter and the exact moment that his body cannot push back, to the point that he has nothing left to do but give in to it.

Does not put his arms up in grand gesture, or cover his head. Does not tuck them to his chest.

Just exhales, and falls to the hay.

ACKNO LEDGE MENTS

With much gratitude:

To John Kenny, for valuable guidance during the project and keen eye on the novel. For also being a farmer's son and knowing what that means.

To Bob Albrecht, for reluctantly agreeing to be my first writing teacher many years ago. More importantly, for the friendship that followed.

To Lorri Dennis, mother and indefatigable cheerleader.

To Brian Langan and his assistance with the business of writing.

To NUI Galway, for the Galway Doctoral Fellowship. For shelter from the rain.

To Sean Campbell and époque press. They took on this book and made it better. A writer can't ask for more.

Thanks to the following for reading drafts of the novel or offering insight:

Martin Keaveney, Adrian Frazier, Stephen Reilly, Ashley Cahillane, Nicki Griffin, Alan McMonagle, John Doherty and Ballyhaise Agricultural College, Ultan Lally, John Carrigy, Mike McCormack, Jonathan Farrar, Jessica Maybury, Þóra Tómasdóttir and StormGeo Sverige.

For helping tell the story of Cúchulainn, much appreciation to The Tàin (1970) by Thomas Kinsella and Cú Chulainn: An Iron Age Hero (2005) by Daragh Smyth and Heather McKay.

And finally:

Soprattutto, a Cerbiatta. Il tuo sostegno ha segnato la transizione da scrittore fallito ad autore.